"SO WHAT'S THE BIG NEWS?" RUTHIE ASKED.

Lucy grinned. "Just the answer to our vacation dilemma. At Habitat today there was an announcement about a dude ranch in Arizona called the Lucky Star."

"A dude ranch, eh?" Reverend Camden asked with a gleam in his eye. He looked wistful. "Now *that* sounds like a vacation!"

The reverend looked at Lucy. "I think we should do it," he said. "The only question is, can we convince the rest of the family?"

7th Heaven™

DUDE RANCH

by Amanda Christie

An Original Novel

Based on the hit TV series
created by Brenda Hampton

Random House ⌂ New York

Cover Background Photograph © Gunter Marx/Corbis

www.randomhouse.com/teens

Library of Congress Control Number: 2001094303
ISBN: 0-375-81431-0

Printed in the United States of America
First Edition
June 2002
10 9 8 7 6 5 4

7th Heaven

DUDE RANCH

ONE

"How about this one?" Ruthie Camden asked. She held up a brochure. On the cover was a picture of an exotic tropical island. The sand on the beach was pure white, and the water was sparkling blue.

Mrs. Camden glanced up. "That looks beautiful, Ruthie, but it's too expensive."

Ruthie frowned. She looked doubtfully at the cover of the brochure. "How can you tell? You barely looked at it!"

"I can tell," said her mom, studying the stack of brochures on the kitchen table.

Ruthie sighed and dropped the island brochure into the NO bag. The NO bag was sitting on the floor between Ruthie's and her mom's chairs. It was almost full.

There goes another one, Ruthie thought. *We're* never *going on vacation!*

For the past couple of weeks, the Camdens had been looking through brochures, combing newspapers, and talking to travel agents. It was the end of the summer, and they wanted to go away on vacation. The trouble was, they couldn't find much they could afford!

Ruthie was picking up another brochure when the kitchen door banged open behind them. Mary and Simon startled their mother as they barged in, laughing.

"Sorry, Mom," Simon said, noticing the tired look on his mother's face. He eased the door shut. "How goes the search?"

"Don't ask," said Ruthie glumly.

"What she said," agreed their mother.

Mary glanced at her little brother. "That good, huh?"

Mary and Simon were dressed in T-shirts, shorts, and sneakers. Simon was holding a basketball, and both he and Mary were dripping with sweat.

Ruthie scrunched her nose. "What smells?"

Simon and Mary looked at each other guiltily. "Um . . . ," said Simon.

"Well . . . ," began Mary.

Ruthie looked shocked. "You mean it's *you guys*?" She shook her head. "If growing up means you start smelling like that, I don't think I *ever* want to grow up."

Mrs. Camden smiled at her daughter, then turned to Simon and Mary. "How'd the game go?"

Mary tousled Simon's hair. "Great, for *one* of us. When did Simon get so tall?"

Simon grinned. "When did you get so slow?" he retorted. He and Mary had played an intense game of one-on-one in the driveway.

"All I know is," Mary continued, "'little brothers are *not* supposed to beat older sisters. Especially not at basketball."

Just then the kitchen door banged open again. "I've got it!" cried Lucy as she charged in.

Mrs. Camden jumped in her seat, then closed her eyes. "I *really* need a vacation," she said.

Matt came through the door behind Lucy. "Sorry, Mom," he said, quietly shutting the door. He set his car keys on the counter as Lucy dropped her bag against the wall. Matt, who was home from medical school for the summer, had just picked Lucy up from a Habitat for Humanity meeting. Lucy was wearing her usual Habitat outfit—old clothes and a bandanna tied over her hair.

"So what's the big news?" Ruthie asked.

Lucy grinned. "Just the answer to our vacation dilemma. Is Dad around?"

"He's in the study," Mrs. Camden said.

Lucy started to rush off. "Wait a minute!" Simon said, blocking her way. "Aren't you going to tell us what it is?"

"I need to run it by Dad first," Lucy replied.

Simon looked at Matt for an explanation. Matt just shrugged. "She wouldn't tell me, either," he said.

Lucy crinkled her nose. "By the way, you guys stink!"

"That's what I said!" crowed Ruthie as Lucy escaped from the kitchen.

Lucy hurried down the hall. If she was right, what she'd learned at Habitat would not only allow them to have an affordable vacation but would also give them a chance to help out some people who really needed it.

Lucy knocked politely at the double doors of her dad's study.

"Come in!" her father called.

Lucy swung open the door and stepped inside. The twins were on the floor playing with Legos. Reverend Camden was sitting at his desk, looking through . . . brochures! He held one up helplessly. "I don't know what to do!" he said.

Lucy closed the door behind her, then sat down in the chair across the desk from her dad.

"We can't really afford any of these vacations," the reverend continued, "but your mother needs a break. We *all* do."

Lucy smiled and leaned forward. "Dad, I think I've got the answer."

Reverend Camden raised his eyebrows. "Really?"

Lucy nodded.

The reverend tossed the brochure he was holding onto the desk and leaned back in his chair. "Do tell."

"At Habitat today there was an announcement about a dude ranch in Arizona called the Lucky Star."

"A dude ranch, eh?" the reverend asked with a gleam in his eye.

Lucy smiled. She'd *thought* her dad would like the idea of a dude ranch. He loved old TV westerns, with cowboys and cattle drives.

"Well, it isn't a dude ranch *yet*," Lucy said quickly. "That's the thing. It's a working ranch, but it's in financial trouble. The Hendersons—that's the family that owns the place—have decided to open it to tourists to make more money."

The reverend looked confused. "So . . . it *isn't* a dude ranch?"

"Not yet," repeated Lucy. "In a way, that's what makes this such an incredible opportunity. You see, the Hendersons need to practice having tourists on the ranch—getting them involved in ranch activities, that kind of thing. We can go and be their test guests!"

The reverend looked intrigued. "How much does it cost?"

"That's the best part," Lucy said. "It's free!"

"Free?"

Lucy nodded. "Well," she said, "it doesn't cost any *money*. . . ."

The reverend just looked at her.

"Remember how I said the ranch was having financial difficulty?" Lucy asked.

Her father nodded.

"It's been in trouble for some time," Lucy explained, "and the place is pretty run-down. The Hendersons need help fixing it up, but they can't pay anybody. . . ."

"I see," said Reverend Camden. "So they put us up and feed us, and in return, we help them with repairs?"

"*And* get to be their test guests," Lucy reminded her father.

The reverend looked doubtful. "I don't know, Luce. It doesn't sound like a vacation."

"Just listen," Lucy said. "Mrs. Henderson's family started the Lucky Star back in 1839! Can you believe that? They've lived there and run the ranch ever since."

"That's really rare," the reverend admitted.

"If they don't get help," Lucy said, "they're going to lose the ranch."

Reverend Camden sighed. "Tell me again what we'll do as their test guests?"

"Everything they do," said Lucy. "We'll feed the animals, go on cattle drives, have cookouts, campfires. . . ."

The reverend looked wistful. "Now *that* sounds like a vacation! And our work will help a family keep their home, a home they've had for almost two hundred years."

The reverend looked at Lucy for a moment. "I think we should do it," he said decisively. "The only question is, can we convince the rest of the family?"

"I'll take Simon, Ruthie, Matt, and Mary," said Lucy.

"And I'll take your mother," said the reverend. Suddenly all the confidence left his face. "Or at least, I'll get started. After you're done, maybe you could swing by and see how I'm doing?"

Lucy smiled. "Will do."

Ten minutes later, Lucy had corralled Matt, Simon, and Ruthie in Simon's room.

"So?" Simon asked. He'd just gotten out of the shower and into clean clothes.

"Yeah, what's the big secret?" Ruthie asked.

"We're all dying to know," added Matt.

Lucy sat down on Simon's bed and explained about the Hendersons and the Lucky Star Ranch.

Ruthie only wanted to know one thing: "Will we get to ride horses?"

"As the Hendersons' test guests, I think we'll do a lot of riding."

"I'm in," Ruthie said. "Later, dudes!" She

waved at them and flounced out the door.

"Meet us down in the kitchen in a few minutes!" Lucy called after her. Then she turned back to Simon and Matt. "Well? What do you say?"

Simon looked thoughtful. "Unlike you, I'm not into carpentry. And unlike Ruthie, I'm not crazy about riding horses. So it doesn't sound like a whole lot of fun to me."

Matt nodded. "I feel the same way. A dude ranch has never been my idea of a good time. On the *other* hand," he said before Lucy could open her mouth to object, "I think it's the *perfect* solution to the vacation problem. It's cheap, we'd be help-ing people, and you *know* Dad's got to love the idea." They all smiled, thinking about the reverend's love of the Old West.

"Wait a minute," said Simon. "Speaking of parents, what is Mom going to think? She really needs a break. Is she going to want to spend her vacation working?"

"And taking care of the twins at the same time?" Matt asked.

Lucy nodded. "I know. Dad's talking to her right now. After I run the idea by Mary, I'm going down to the kitchen to help him out."

"You'll never get Mary to go along with it," Simon said.

"You may be right," Matt said thoughtfully. "But maybe not."

Lucy gave him a questioning look.

"I've got an idea," Matt explained. "Why don't you let me talk to Mary, and I'll see what I can do?"

"What's your idea?" Lucy asked.

Matt grinned. "I think I'll keep it to myself for the time being," he said.

Simon snickered at the look on Lucy's face. "Well, whether you convince Mom or not, I don't think I really want to go."

"Simon, you *have* to!" Lucy said.

"Yeah," Matt agreed. "If you don't, you're just giving Mom an excuse to bail, too."

Simon shrugged.

Lucy's shoulders slumped in defeat, but Matt had an idea.

"You like puzzles, right, Simon?" Matt asked.

Simon nodded.

"And we know you're interested in money."

"Who isn't?" Simon asked.

"Good point," said Matt. He turned to

Lucy. "Didn't you say that the ranch had been around since the 1800s?"

"That's right," Lucy said. "The ranch was started in 1839 and passed down through the generations."

"1839 . . . ," Matt mused. "It's been a while since I've taken American history, but wasn't Arizona full of gold mines back then?"

"Sure," Lucy said.

Simon was nodding, too. "So what?"

"*So* . . . ," said Matt, "that was a pretty rough time. Didn't a lot of the old miners bury what they found to hide it from other miners?"

"That's right!" Lucy said, suddenly seeing where Matt was going. "And some people think that there's gold still stashed in the hills, just waiting for someone clever enough to find it. . . ."

Simon looked thoughtful. "I guess I could do some research on the Web, see what kind of clues I can turn up. . . ."

Lucy held her breath as a smile spread across Simon's face. He nodded at his sister and brother. "Okay, you've got me!" he said. "How can I resist gold *and* intrigue?"

"That's what I was counting on," Matt said with a grin.

"In fact," Simon went on, "the Hendersons are having money trouble, right?" Lucy nodded. "If I manage to find anything, I'll turn it over to them. That'll be my way of helping the ranch."

"Wow," Lucy said. "That's a great idea!"

Simon grinned. "What can I say? I'm a genius."

Lucy and Matt exchanged glances. *Oh, brother!* Lucy thought.

Just then the bedroom door opened and Mary stuck her head in. She was wet, but clean. Her hair was wrapped in a towel, and she was wearing her bathrobe.

"Ruthie said you guys were looking for me?" she asked.

Matt stood up. "Leave this to me," he said to Lucy.

Lucy gave her older brother a big smile. "Thanks, Matt. Remember, kitchen in five minutes," she said.

"Gotcha!" said Matt. He took Mary's arm and started down the hall. "It's about our vacation . . . ," he began.

TWO

"*No way!*" Mrs. Camden exclaimed.

Reverend and Mrs. Camden, Simon, Lucy, and Ruthie were sitting around the kitchen table. The twins had followed their father in and were sitting on the floor, once again surrounded by Legos.

"I work every day of my life," Mrs. Camden continued. "Why would I want to work on vacation?"

Simon looked at Lucy as if to say, *I told you.*

"Because it's for a good cause, Mom," said Lucy. "Besides, it'll end up being a lot of fun."

Simon jumped in. "I'll bet there's great

stuff you could do to help out, Mom."

"That's right," said the reverend. "I'm sure the Hendersons need help decorating the interiors of the bunkhouses. You *love* to decorate."

"Yeah," said Simon. "They'll have to be really nice, now that tourists will be staying in them instead of ranch hands."

"Come on, Mom," Ruthie said, "be a dude!"

Mrs. Camden gave her youngest daughter a wry smile. "What about the boys? Who's going to take care of them while we're out fixing up bunkhouses and riding the range?"

"We'll take care of that," Mary said, walking into the room with Matt.

Matt grinned. "Mary and I have decided to stick around here and watch the twins."

Mary reached down and tousled David's hair. "We need some bonding time. Kids grow up so fast!"

"Are you sure?" Mrs. Camden asked. "You two deserve a vacation, too."

"Sure we're sure!" Mary said, giving her mom a big smile.

Mrs. Camden raised an eyebrow. "You

don't have any other reason to stay home that I should know about, do you?"

Mary's smile faltered. "Well . . . ," she said.

Mrs. Camden crossed her arms over her chest. "I thought so. Spill it!"

"Ah . . ." Mary looked at Matt for help.

Matt frowned and clasped his hands. "Well . . . since there isn't going to be anybody around, Mary and I thought we might have some people over to the house for a little party—"

"Great idea!" the reverend said, springing to his feet. "Of *course* you should have people over!"

"Of course?" Mrs. Camden said dubiously.

"Absolutely!" exclaimed the reverend.

"How many people?" Mrs. Camden wanted to know.

Mary and Matt looked at each other. "A dozen?" Matt said tentatively.

"Perfect!" said the reverend.

Simon interrupted, "Wow, Dad. You *really* want to be a cowboy, don't you? Imagine, letting Matt and Mary take care of the twins *and* throw a party."

Mrs. Camden was shaking her head and opening her mouth to say something when Mary jumped in.

"Mom, we'll be really responsible. We won't let it get too loud, and we'll have everybody out early."

Lucy spoke up. "Makes sense to me," she said. "Matt and Mary will be having fun here at home while we're having fun at the ranch. That way, everybody gets a little vacation."

Mrs. Camden looked around at all their faces, then sighed. "All right," she said.

Ruthie pumped her fist. "Yes!"

"Hold your horses, young lady!" Mrs. Camden said. She turned to Lucy. "What's the next step?"

"At the Habitat meeting we were told that the Hendersons need people anytime."

Mrs. Camden sat back in her chair. "I think I'll let you guys take care of the details. Just let me know when to have my bags packed."

The reverend patted his wife's arm. "You'll see," he said. "Riding the range, roping dogies . . . This is going to be the best vacation ever!"

• • •

Just a week later, the Camdens turned onto a dirt road marked by a sign reading LUCKY STAR RANCH.

"Here we are!" announced the reverend from the driver's seat.

"Dude!" Ruthie called from the back.

Lucy groaned. For the last week, Ruthie had taken every opportunity to use that word.

"Look!" Simon said. He was pointing to the sign. Above the word RANCH someone had written DUDE in white spray paint.

"I guess that's what it is now," said the reverend.

But Lucy couldn't shake the feeling that whoever had written DUDE hadn't meant it in a nice way.

As they drove along the road, Lucy noticed the land. During the last hour of their trip, it had grown flat—and red! Lucy had the strange feeling that she had somehow traveled to Mars. In the distance, she could see stone mesas one after the other against the horizon.

Mrs. Camden rolled down her window, and they were hit by a blast of hot, dry air.

Lucy was surprised by how pleasant it felt.

"No humidity!" Mrs. Camden called.

The Camdens topped a slight rise and saw the ranch ahead. It had been built in the shadow of the nearest mesa. Lucy could see a barn, a house, and several small, low buildings. There were a number of corrals, as well, with horses grazing and tossing their heads.

"Cool!" said Ruthie.

Mrs. Camden smiled back at them. "I think maybe you guys were right. This is going to be a great vacation."

As they got closer to the ranch, however, the excitement in the car began to dim. The small buildings on the outskirts of the ranch looked abandoned. They were missing doors and windows. Their walls were cracked and peeling, as if they hadn't been painted in years.

Lucy shook her head. "There's a lot to do here."

Nearer to the center of the ranch, things looked a little better. The main house had been recently painted, and there were people painting the barn.

Lucy rolled down her window and stuck her head out. The dry air lifted her hair.

"The roof on the main house looks new," she reported.

As they pulled up in front of the house, a fair-haired boy about Ruthie's age jumped up from the porch steps and ran into the house, which was two stories tall and looked quite large. A long porch ran the length of the house on two sides.

"Well, hello, Camdens!" called a lanky gentleman who was coming out of the house. The man wore a western-style shirt with jeans and boots. On his head was a broad-brimmed cowboy hat. His face was lined and his hair white, but his eyes were a bright, lively blue.

"Welcome to the Lucky Star," the man said. "I'm Cal Henderson."

Reverend Camden looked a little star-struck. Lucy grinned and elbowed Simon. "He's meeting a *real cowboy*!" she said under her breath.

"Nice to meet you, Mr. Henderson," said the reverend, extending his hand. "And thank you so much for having us."

"Not at'all," said Mr. Henderson, "not at'all. Y'all are doing us a big favor by coming and helping out." He turned toward Mrs. Camden.

"And this lovely lady must be your wife." Mr. Henderson doffed his hat. "Mrs. Camden, it's a pleasure to have you here at the Lucky Star."

Lucy couldn't believe it. Her mom was blushing!

"Why, thank you, Mr. Henderson," said Mrs. Camden. "I understand this ranch has been in your family for generations."

"Almost two hundred years!" someone said. Lucy looked over to see a slender older woman in a flowered dress coming through the screened front door.

Mr. Henderson smiled. "This is my wife, Rachel."

"And it's my family, not his, that started this ranch," said Mrs. Henderson, coming down the porch steps. "Don't let him tell you otherwise!"

Mr. Henderson nodded. "That's true. I married into this great ranching family."

Mrs. Henderson came up beside her husband and smiled at the Camdens. Her gray hair was pulled neatly back in a bun. "Mighty nice to have you folks here," she said. "We appreciate all the help we can get. In return, I hope we can show you a good time."

"I'm already having a good time," said

the reverend, wearing a goofy smile.

"Ignore him," said Mrs. Camden. "He's just a little overenthusiastic. Let me introduce my children. This is Simon, and Lucy," Mrs. Camden continued.

"I understand we have you to thank for your family's being here," said Mr. Henderson as he and Lucy shook hands.

"Not really," Lucy said modestly. "I just heard you needed some help."

"And finally," Annie concluded, "my youngest daughter, Ruthie."

"Hey!" Ruthie said.

"Well, hello there!" said Mrs. Henderson, squinting down at Ruthie as if thinking something over. "Unless I'm mistaken," she said, "this here's a little girl who belongs on horseback."

Ruthie grinned. "Yeah! I mean, you're not mistaken."

Mrs. Henderson nodded judiciously. "It's almost time for lunch, but after that, I'll have Cody show you the stable."

"Cody's our younger boy," explained Mr. Henderson.

"I didn't know you had children," said Mrs. Camden.

"Oh, yes," said Mrs. Henderson. "Two

boys. And they'll be the death of me yet!"

"Cody is just about Ruthie's age, I bet," Mr. Henderson said. Then he turned to Lucy. "Are you still in high school?"

"I just finished my first year of college," Lucy said.

"My older son, Luke, just graduated from high school," said Mr. Henderson. "Well . . . he wasn't attending high school, exactly. What I mean is—"

"What my husband is trying to say," broke in Mrs. Henderson, "is that Luke has been homeschooled these last four years."

"Homeschooled?" Mrs. Camden said. "I have a lot of respect for homeschooling. In many ways, I think the child gets a better education."

Mrs. Henderson pursed her lips. "Maybe," she said.

Mr. Henderson laughed—a little uneasily, Lucy thought. "Why don't we show you the house and your bedrooms, and you can get settled?"

"That would be great," said the reverend.

Everyone grabbed a bag and followed Mrs. Henderson up the porch steps. The screen door creaked as she pulled it open and walked into the hallway beyond. To the right of the door was a narrow flight of wooden stairs.

"Just drop your bags there by the stairs, then head straight on through!" called Mr. Henderson from the back of the group.

The Camdens headed down the short, narrow hall into a low, warm room with a stone fireplace. In front of the fireplace was a bearskin rug, complete with head and paws! The bear skin looked old and had no fur in spots. There was a worn leather couch in the middle of the room. On either side of the couch were wooden end tables. The lamps on the tables were made from the bleached skulls of cattle! Against one wall was a glass case full of trophies and ribbons. Above the case were framed photos. There didn't seem to be a TV in the room.

"This is the family room," Mr. Henderson explained. "For reading, relaxing, chitchat, or whatever you feel like."

The reverend had wandered over to the trophy case. "I see that your boys do some riding in rodeos."

Mr. Henderson smiled proudly. "Luke takes after his mother. She's still one of the best darned cowhands in the whole state! Luke was ranked fourth in his age group, before he—" Mr. Henderson broke off suddenly. "—when he was younger," he concluded.

"How about Cody?" Mrs. Camden inquired pleasantly.

"Oh, he takes after his father," said Mrs. Henderson.

Mr. Henderson hooked his thumbs in his belt and rocked back on his heels. "True, true. When I was a boy, I was always looking under rocks for snakes and bringing home turtles. Cody's just the same way."

"Sounds like someone I'd like to meet," said Ruthie.

Mrs. Henderson put her hands on her hips and looked around with sharp eyes. "Where *are* those boys?" she asked.

"Oh, they're around," said Mr. Henderson. "Probably just a little shy."

"*Hmph!*" huffed Mrs. Henderson. "Anyway, through here is the dining room. . . ."

Everyone followed Mrs. Henderson across the hall to a large room with a long, wide table in the center. There were several volunteers working. Lucy noted with interest that they were putting up a new wall.

"As you can see," said Mrs. Henderson, "we're making this room larger. The kitchen's on the other side of that new wall."

"Since we're right here, why don't you stay and start lunch?" Mr. Henderson suggested to his wife. "I can take these folks upstairs and show them their rooms."

The Camdens followed Mr. Henderson back down the hall to the stairs. They picked up their bags and started single file up the steps, which creaked and moaned.

Mr. Henderson shook his head. "This staircase is something else that needs fixing," he said. "It's too narrow. We need to make it wider."

Lucy nodded. That would certainly be a fun project!

At the top of the steps was a long hall with doors opening off of it.

"The missus and I have our bedroom downstairs, next to the kitchen," explained Mr. Henderson. "So do the boys. We used to sleep up here, but now these will all be guest bedrooms."

"That must have been hard on your boys," said Mrs. Camden. "Giving up their bedrooms."

Mr. Henderson shrugged. "We've all had to get used to some changes."

Just then Ruthie called out, "I'd like this

room!" She had gone on ahead and poked her head into a few rooms.

Mr. Henderson smiled. "I *thought* your little girl would like that room." The group moved down the hall and looked in.

Ruthie was lying on a big four-poster bed with a gauzy canopy suspended above. On the walls were framed pictures of horses, and there were horse figurines on top of the dresser. Lucy smiled. It was the perfect room for her sister.

"Now, Simon," said Mr. Henderson. "Your room is the next door down. Lucy, your room is beside your brother's. And Reverend and Mrs. Camden, you're across the hall from Lucy."

"Thank you," said the reverend.

Mr. Henderson touched the brim of his hat and nodded. "Y'all just give a holler if you need anything. Lunch'll be ready shortly." Then he turned and started down the steps, his boots knocking hollowly against the wood.

Lucy went down the hall and dropped her bag in her room. It was nice, with a large window on the far wall letting in lots of golden afternoon light. The room was decorated in a western style: hanging on the wall were different shapes and styles of spurs, and arranged in the corner was a coiled rope.

Lucy unpacked quickly, then walked down the hall to Simon's room. He was sitting at a desk, setting up his laptop.

"They must have installed new phone lines," Simon said. "There's a modem jack built right in."

"Why'd you bring your laptop?" Lucy asked. "You're not going to be day trading while we're here, are you?"

Simon shook his head. "I bookmarked a bunch of different sites about Arizona gold mines before we left. I just want to pull them up and review them."

"Any leads?" Lucy asked, interested.

Simon shrugged. "Some tantalizing stories, but I'm not sure they're *leads*. I'm hoping the Hendersons will have some ideas."

A bell rang downstairs. The reverend appeared in the doorway. "I believe that's the dinner bell," he said.

"Dad, don't you mean *lunch* bell?" Lucy asked.

"Lunch, dinner . . . it's all grub! Come on, let's go chow down!"

As the reverend headed down the stairs,

Lucy looked at Simon. *Grub?* she mouthed. Simon just smiled and shook his head.

"Let's go, kids," their mother said on her way past. "Let's not keep our hosts waiting."

Downstairs, a small crowd had gathered in the dining room. Sweaty, dusty men and women milled around, talking and laughing. Lucy wondered if these were all guests of the ranch, like the Camdens were, or if they were just local volunteers who'd come in for the day. She was scanning the group when someone stepped to the side and she got a look at . . .

Lucy felt her stomach drop. She swallowed. Standing on the other side of the table was a boy about her age. He had dark hair and dark eyes and was wearing a T-shirt and jeans. He was listening intently to something one of the volunteers was saying, a smile playing about his lips. He was *very* rugged and attractive.

Mr. Henderson stepped in from the kitchen and stood at the head of the table. He lifted his arms. "All right, everybody! If I could get your attention! I just wanted to thank everyone again for being here and helping us fix up the place. You know it means the world to us. I also wanted to announce the arrival of our first guests at the Lucky Star Dude Ranch, the Reverend and Mrs. Camden and their children Lucy, Simon, and Ruthie!"

Mr. Henderson gestured toward the Camdens, and everyone around the table cheered and applauded. Lucy smiled at all the open, welcoming faces around her . . . all except one. The dark-haired boy wasn't smiling. He wasn't clapping, either. He was staring at Lucy with a look of pure hatred.

THREE

Startled, Lucy dropped her eyes . . . and found herself staring at the boy's right hand, which was resting lightly on the table.

Despite herself, Lucy felt a moment of shock. There was something very wrong with his hand. It looked as though he was missing almost all of his fingers, and the skin on the hand was red and rough.

Lucy glanced back up at the boy's face. If he had been angry before, he was furious now. Holding Lucy's gaze, he slowly raised his mutilated hand, as if to give Lucy a good look at the damage. She saw that the boy still had his thumb but that his first finger was missing its tip. The other fingers were mere stumps.

Lucy looked away. Coming through the door from the kitchen was the fair-haired boy they'd seen when they'd first pulled up. He was carrying a plate loaded with sandwiches. Behind him came Mr. Henderson, carrying pitchers of lemonade.

The boy slowly moved around the table, letting each person choose a sandwich. Mr. Henderson followed, pouring drinks. Eventually, Mrs. Henderson came out of the kitchen to an appreciative greeting from everyone eating.

"Don't waste time talking to me," she said. "Eat up!"

Lucy did as she was told. She didn't look back at the dark-haired boy for the entire lunch. She was angry at herself for the way his hand had shocked her. Even worse, she'd let him *see* that shock! She suddenly felt compassion for the boy. No wonder he was so angry, she thought. He must hate dealing with stares all the time.

Lucy wondered how it had happened. Had he been born that way? Or had there been some terrible accident?

After lunch, Mr. Henderson asked the Camdens to join him in the family room. While the rest of the volunteers got back to work, Lucy and her family plopped down on the leather couch and low canvas chairs.

Mr. Henderson stood at the front of the room. "Okay, Camdens," he said. "Now's when we figure out what you want to do to help out around here, or what you *can* do."

"Anything," Lucy said.

Everyone laughed. "Lucy really loves carpentry," Mrs. Camden explained.

"Perfect!" Mr. Henderson said. "Lucy, you can help with any number of ongoing projects."

"How about the wall going up in the dining room?" Lucy asked.

"I don't see why not," Mr. Henderson answered. "Who else?"

Mrs. Camden spoke up. "Is there work to be done on the bunkhouses?"

Mr. Henderson tipped back his hat. "Well, ma'am, here I'd been figuring you'd be our dough puncher."

"Dough puncher?" Mrs. Camden said. "That sounds interesting. What's the dough puncher do?"

Now Mr. Henderson looked uncomfortable. "The dough puncher, ma'am, is the cook."

Mrs. Camden's eyes grew wide, then she started laughing. "I'm sorry, Mr. Henderson, but I'm going to have to pass that job on to someone else. I cook every day at home. I'd much rather work on a construction project."

"Well . . . ," Mr. Henderson said, "there *is* a team working on one of the bunkhouses. We're converting them into guest houses. You can join them."

"Just what I was hoping," Mrs. Camden said.

"But we can't leave Mr. Henderson without a dough puncher," the reverend said, concerned. "Who's going to do that?"

Reverend Camden looked from one family member to another. Everyone stared right back at him!

"Simon!" the reverend said desperately.

"Oh, no," Simon said, shaking his head. He turned to Mr. Henderson. "When we came in, I noticed there were people painting the barn. Do you think they could use some help?"

"I'm sure they could, Simon," Mr. Henderson said. "I believe there's a paintbrush with your name on it!"

"What about me?" Ruthie asked.

Mr. Henderson planted his hands on his hips and looked down at Ruthie. "Well, what do you want to do, young lady?"

Ruthie shrugged. "Something with the horses would be great."

Mr. Henderson considered. "Well, there's always work to do there. I'm sure our horse wrangler, Shelly, could use a hand."

Ruthie grinned. "Awesome, dude!"

Reverend Camden raised his hands in defeat. "I guess that leaves me with the dough punching."

Mr. Henderson stifled a smile. "I'm afraid it does at that, sir."

Mrs. Camden grinned. "Oh, it won't be so bad," she said. "Maybe you'll learn something."

The reverend groaned.

Now Mr. Henderson was smiling openly. "Well, the only thing left to talk about is the ranching part of your stay here. That means, whatever we normally do in running the ranch, you'll all participate in."

The reverend sat up eagerly. "When's the cattle drive?" he asked.

"The day after tomorrow," said Mr. Henderson.

"Will we be roping dogies?" the reverend asked.

Ruthie slapped a hand to her forehead. Simon rolled his eyes. "Dad!"

"What?" the reverend asked.

"If there are dogies to be roped," Mr. Henderson said, "you'll be roping them. Tomorrow we'll take a trip out to the north pasture to feed the herd. You're also welcome to help feed and tend to the horses.

"Of course," continued Mr. Henderson, "you can all do as much or as little as you like. That's what being a guest at this ranch is all about right now."

"Thank you, Mr. Henderson, but we very much want to help you get on your feet," said Mrs. Camden. "Plus, I think we're all very excited about riding horses and exploring this beautiful country."

Mr. Henderson bowed slightly. "Thank you, ma'am."

Suddenly Mr. Henderson grinned in the direction of the door. "Cody! Where have you been hiding? Come on in here and say hello to our guests. Camdens, this here is my younger son, Cody."

The fair-haired boy they had seen at

lunch was standing in the doorway. He grinned at everybody and said, "Hey."

"Hey," Ruthie said right back. Cody looked at her and smiled.

Lucy raised an eyebrow. *Since when is my little sister interested in boys?* she thought.

Mr. Henderson introduced each of the Camdens. When he got to Ruthie, he said, "Ruthie is going to be helping Shelly with the horses. Cody, why don't you take her down to the stable and introduce her for me?"

"Sure, Dad," Cody said. He smiled at Ruthie, this time a little more shyly. "Would you like to meet my horse?"

"Sure," Ruthie said, a little shy herself. Lucy couldn't believe her eyes. Since when was Ruthie shy?

"What's his name?" Ruthie asked, joining Cody at the door.

"Gold Dust," Cody said, "but we call him Dusty for short."

"Well," the reverend said as Cody and Ruthie left the room, "I suppose we'd better get to work. I'll report to the kitchen, as ordered."

"And I'm off to the bunkhouse!" Mrs.

Camden said. She looked excited.

"Y'all have fun," Mr. Henderson said.

Lucy quickly ran upstairs and changed into work clothes, then joined the volunteers working on the wall. She spent the next couple of hours deeply absorbed in what she was doing. When one of the other volunteers finally called a halt, Lucy couldn't believe how much time had passed. It had felt like minutes, not hours!

They stood back to admire their work. The wall was almost finished. Lucy figured they'd be able to complete it tomorrow. Then she'd have to find more work!

Her fellow workers lived in the area and were going home for the evening. Lucy said goodbye and walked outside for a breath of fresh air. Evening was coming on, and the sky reflected the redness of the huge, empty land. The air was still hot; Lucy could feel it filling her lungs.

A little work, a little beauty . . . *This* was what Lucy called a vacation!

Thinking she might check in with Ruthie, Lucy wandered down to the stable. Through the middle of the low structure was a long, open passage. On either side of the passage were stalls. It was dim inside, and quiet. She could hear the shufflings and snorts of horses.

Lucy wandered to the end of the passage and looked outside. A bunch of volunteers and hands were sitting on the corral fence, cheering and hollering. Inside the corral, a horse was spinning in tight circles, kicking up a haze of red dust. A rider in a black cowboy hat was clinging to the horse's back. In the twilight, Lucy couldn't make out who it was.

"Go! Go!" the crowd yelled.

Lucy drifted toward the corral. She watched the rider, amazed. No matter how hard the horse twisted or bucked, the rider clung on. He wasn't even using a saddle, just riding bareback! It was as though he were part of the horse.

After a few more minutes of struggle, the horse seemed to tire. The rider walked the horse in larger and larger circles. He was leaning close to the horse's head.

The people on the fence began to call out their congratulations and wander off. A few of them greeted Lucy with warm smiles as they passed.

Lucy waited and then walked over to the fence. Even before she could see him clearly, she felt sure who the rider would be.

From the fence she watched as the boy with the injured hand dismounted in the middle of the ring. Talking softly to the horse, he led it toward the gate. Lucy noticed that he used his injured hand easily, switching hands quickly at certain moments and using his arm, as well as his good hand, to hold things.

"That was incredible," Lucy said when the boy reached the fence. "How'd you learn to do that?"

Surprised, the boy looked up. Obviously, he hadn't noticed Lucy standing there in the fading light.

When he saw who it was, his mouth hardened. He opened the gate, walked the horse through, then closed the gate behind him. He started leading the horse to the stable. With a start, Lucy realized she'd just been ignored!

I shouldn't be surprised, she thought, *after the way I stared at his hand at lunch. I'll try again.* She sighed and followed the boy and his horse.

In the stable, the boy flicked on bright overhead lights. In the harsh fluorescent glare, his dark hair and eyes stood out sharply. Lucy thought he was strikingly handsome.

But the lights also clearly illuminated the gruesome scars on the boy's hand. The skin looked as though it had healed unevenly; it was thin in some places, thick in others.

Lucy felt an odd twisting sensation in her stomach. *It's just a hand,* she told herself. *Why am I acting so silly?*

The boy led his horse down the middle of the aisle and hooked its bridle to lead ropes attached to either wall. Again Lucy noticed how easily he worked with his injured hand, using his teeth to hold a strap while his good hand tightened a buckle.

Ruthie and Cody emerged from a stall, where Cody had been introducing Ruthie to Dusty.

"Do you need any help?" Ruthie asked the older boy.

The boy stiffened, and his face grew hard again. Lucy realized that he was assuming she'd asked because of his hand.

"She really loves horses," Lucy quickly said. "You'd be doing her a favor."

The boy glanced back at Ruthie, then

looked at Lucy. "Suit yourself," he said.

"Thanks!" Ruthie said. She went over to the wall and grabbed a step stool. Then she set it down near the horse's head, climbed up, and began to remove the horse's bridle.

"Careful!" the boy warned. "This horse is still a little skittish. Move slowly, unless you want to get kicked."

"Gotcha," Ruthie said. She talked softly to the horse while she loosened the buckles on the bridle.

Lucy glanced into Dusty's stall. Cody had gone back inside and was brushing and talking to his horse. Lucy took a deep breath. *Now's as good a time as any,* she thought.

She stepped forward and cleared her throat. "My name's Lucy," she said.

The boy took the bridle from Ruthie and rested it on a rack on the wall of the passage. "I know," he said. "I was at lunch. Remember?"

He gave Lucy a meaningful look. Lucy blushed, remembering all over again how he'd seen her stare at his hand.

"I owe you an apology," she said. The boy picked up a towel and began rubbing the horse down. "I was just surprised—I mean,

I didn't expect—" Lucy sighed. Was she just making it worse?

The boy tossed the towel into a bin against the wall. "Forget it," the boy said, still not looking at Lucy.

Ruthie still stood on the stool next to the horse. "Can I feed him a carrot?" Ruthie asked the boy.

The boy considered her, then nodded. "Just be careful. Make sure you hold your hand flat."

Ruthie ran over to a bin at the end of the passage and pulled out a carrot. She skipped back and stood close to the horse. "Are you hungry?" Ruthie asked. She held the carrot up to the horse's nose. Its big, velvety nostrils flared over the carrot, then its lips reached to lift it off of Ruthie's palm. Ruthie giggled.

"I like him," she said. "He's a good horse. He's just a little young."

The boy again considered Ruthie for a moment, then turned and called out, "Cody!"

Cody's face appeared in the door to Dusty's stall.

"Come and curry this horse, then put him back in his stall."

"Okay," Cody said. He went to a box

along the side of the passage where various brushes and combs were kept. He selected a couple and brought them back.

"Ruthie," the boy said, "you can help him, if you'd like."

"Thanks! I'd love to," Ruthie said. She took the curry comb from Cody and began brushing the horse with large, circular strokes.

The older boy went to the wall of the passage and lifted the bridle from its rack. He threw it over his shoulder and walked down the passage back toward the house.

Lucy stood there, rooted to the spot. She felt bewildered and a little angry. She'd just tried to apologize, and the boy had basically ignored her again!

"Don't let it bother you," Cody said as he brushed the horse. "My brother's got some issues."

His brother? Of course! Lucy thought. So that was the older Henderson boy, the one who'd won all those trophies and ribbons in the trophy case, the one who'd been homeschooled through high school.

Suddenly Lucy recalled how Mr. Henderson had had trouble talking about his older son. What had he said? His older son,

Luke, had been ranked fourth in the state at the rodeos, until . . .

Until something had happened to his hand? Lucy wondered. She looked after Luke, her mouth settling into a firm line. No wonder the boy was angry. Lucy could only guess how hard it had been for him. But did that excuse his rude behavior? Lucy didn't know what to think.

FOUR

"Ah-choo!" Simon's sneeze blew away the dust that covered the yellowed parchment in his hands.

Half an hour ago, they'd stopped work on painting the barn. Simon had cleaned up and gone in search of Mr. or Mrs. Henderson. He hoped one of them would be able to add to what he'd discovered on the Web about Arizona gold mines and forgotten gold.

He'd found Mrs. Henderson—and his dad!—hard at work in the kitchen, preparing dinner. Simon was surprised to see that the reverend was very involved in his work. He was wearing a large white apron that said CAN I COOK, OR WHAT?

When Simon entered the kitchen, the reverend glanced up briefly. "Oh, hi, son," he said distractedly before turning back to whatever he had bubbling on the stove.

Simon asked Mrs. Henderson about the gold. She frowned, deep in thought.

"Well, Simon," she said, "there are plenty of stories, but nothing I know for sure. Why don't you look in our den? There are all sorts of old letters there, dating back from when my family first founded this ranch." Mrs. Henderson gave Simon a mischievous grin. "You never know what you'll find there!"

Simon had found the den at the back of the house, next to the Hendersons' bedroom. Against one wall there was a desk and a filing cabinet, which he left alone. The other walls were taken up by bookshelves, crammed full of old books, photo albums, and letters.

Simon had spent the last hour reading through old records of cattle bought and sold, calves birthed, cows that died of sickness. There were also ancient ledgers tracking money borrowed, owed, and paid back. Simon was quickly learning that for most of its history, the ranch had operated in debt, narrowly avoiding bankruptcy. So what the Hendersons were experiencing now was nothing new.

Simon wondered why the family would keep at it all these years if it was so difficult. Then he answered himself: *Because they love it—the land, the cattle, the way of life.*

A lot of the stuff Simon was finding was from the 1880s and 1890s. It was interesting to see such old papers, and if he weren't searching for something else, he'd spend more time with them.

But so far, he hadn't found a word about any secret stashes of gold. Until this . . .

Simon held a personal letter. It was written in beautiful script. The ink had faded but was still legible. What had caught Simon's eye was the word *treasure*.

The letter was dated August 16, 1898.

My Dearest Beatrice,

Once again, we are in danger of losing the ranch, and once again we are forced to sell what we can to pay our debts. It is a hateful process, and I dearly hope that you will never have to experience it. I have given up so much, and it seems it is never enough.

One thing I have been able to save, my

dear, is our family's most precious heirloom, which you so admired when you last visited the Lucky Star. Jackson has pressed me to sell it, but I know that I cannot. Still, I worry that, with the best intentions, he will act without my approval. So I have hidden this great treasure where only you will be able to find it.

Begin your search at Rattlesnake Rock, where you and I have spent so many pleasurable hours together. What you find there will take you to the next step. As you follow these instructions, think back on your last visit with us, and I know you will discover the prize.

Until next we meet, I remain,

Your loving Aunt

Simon could scarcely believe his eyes! This was the real thing! But it appeared that the letter had never been sent—so the treasure could still be out there!

Simon's next step was to discover what, and where, Rattlesnake Rock was. He had to assume it was somewhere on the ranch, since Beatrice's aunt had encouraged her to remember her visits while she searched.

Simon heard a bell ring—dinner! He'd been so involved in his search, he hadn't realized how famished he was. Simon carefully returned the letter to the bookshelf where he'd found it. He'd come back later and copy it onto his laptop.

When he got to the dining room, he found his mother and Lucy already at the table, deep in discussion about the day's work. Mrs. Camden was obviously excited, speaking with animation about the reconstruction of the bunkhouse.

Lucy was listening intently and offering suggestions.

Ruthie and Cody came in next.

"Ruthie, you smell like horses," Simon teased. She really did!

"I'm glad," Ruthie said tartly. "It means I spent all day with them. It was great! Cody introduced me to Shelly—she's the horse wrangler. I helped her all day, feeding and brushing the horses."

Cody spoke up. "And don't forget mucking out the stalls," he said.

Ruthie wrinkled her nose. "I was *trying* to forget that part," she said. "I met Cody's pony, Dusty. He's so sweet! Oh, and then Luke was working with a new horse in the corral. I helped to take off the horse's bridle and rub him down."

"Speak of the devil," Simon said as

Luke walked into the room and looked quickly around. Simon saw that Lucy noticed the boy immediately. She was still talking to their mom, but her attention was definitely divided now.

Luke didn't meet anyone's eyes. He sat down near the head of the table without saying a word.

Mr. Henderson poked his head out of the kitchen. "Cody? Would you mind helping us bring in the food?"

Cody got up and went to the kitchen. Simon and Ruthie sat down next to Luke, across the table from Lucy and Mrs. Camden.

Mrs. Camden turned a smiling face toward Simon. "How was your day?" she asked.

Simon gave a brief report of his painting. It was fun, although hot, tiring work in the sun, and he'd met some nice people. He was starting to tell her and Lucy—although Lucy kept glancing at Luke—about the letter he'd found when his mom interrupted.

"I'm sorry, Simon." She turned to the boy near the head of the table. "You must be Luke," she said. "You came in so quietly, and I'm so excited about working on the ranch, that I didn't see you. We didn't have a chance to meet before."

Mrs. Camden stretched her hand across the table. "My name is Annie Camden. These are my children, Simon, Lucy, and Ruthie, who I hear you've already met."

Luke sat as still as stone, staring at their mother's hand. He grimaced slightly, then said, "It's a pleasure to meet you, ma'am."

Mrs. Camden hesitated, then put her hand down. "It's very nice to meet you," she said uncertainly.

"Luke!"

They all jumped. Standing in the doorway to the kitchen was Mrs. Henderson. Her face was red, and Simon didn't think that it was from standing over a hot stove.

"Stand up and shake Mrs. Camden's hand like the gentleman I know you are!" she scolded.

Luke's face flushed a deep shade of red. They all squirmed uncomfortably. Their mom started to say, "Really, Mrs. Henderson, it isn't necessary—"

But before she could finish, Luke pushed back his chair. It made a scraping noise against the wood floor. He stood and looked their mother squarely in the eye.

"It's a pleasure to meet you, ma'am," he said, and stretched out his right hand.

It was only then that Simon noticed how damaged Luke's hand was. *No wonder he didn't want to shake Mom's hand,* Simon thought.

Mrs. Camden glanced at Luke's hand. A flicker of emotion passed over her face but was quickly replaced by respect and seriousness. She reached out and wrapped her hand around Luke's.

"It's always a pleasure to meet a fine young man," she said.

Mrs. Henderson nodded curtly. "Dinner is served," she said, and disappeared back into the kitchen.

FIVE

Lucy felt Luke's embarrassment at being reprimanded by his mother in front of guests. She didn't know what to do with herself throughout dinner. She wanted to talk to Luke, but what could she say? He refused to make conversation or even look up.

Dinner was a much different affair from lunch. All the hands and volunteers had gone to their own homes for the night, so it was just the Hendersons and the Camdens. It was nice and cozy. Lucy found that she liked the Hendersons very much and was glad both to be their guest and to be helping them save their ranch.

Reverend Camden had helped bring in

the food and now was glowing like a proud mother as everyone ate and commented appreciatively.

"I can't really take any credit," he said modestly. "Mrs. Henderson is the head chef. I'm just the dough puncher."

"And a fine dough puncher you are, Reverend Camden!" said Mrs. Henderson. She winked at Mrs. Camden. "Who knows? After your time with us, the Camden kitchen may never be the same again."

Everyone chatted about what they'd done during the day, going back over the work they'd accomplished.

"I can't tell y'all how happy it makes me that you're enjoying helping out," said Mr. Henderson. "You're such nice people. It's a real pleasure to have you here."

"The pleasure is ours," said Mrs. Camden. "I just hope we can get you that much closer to opening to tourists in the fall."

Lucy noticed Luke flinch across the table from her.

"Speaking of which," the reverend said with a gleam in his eye, "what kind of ranch activities can we take part in tomorrow?"

Mr. Henderson laughed. "You'll want to

get a good night's rest because life on the ranch starts early!"

"Before sunrise," Luke offered snidely.

Mr. Henderson ignored Luke's tone. "That's right. First we get up and feed and water the horses."

"Yeah!" Ruthie chimed in.

Mr. Henderson winked at her. "Then we load up the truck with hay from the barn and drive out to the pasture, where we feed the cattle. After that, we'll come back here," Mr. Henderson continued. "Y'all can either join back in with the volunteers or take some time off."

"Sounds fun," Simon said.

"Sure does," Lucy agreed. They were going to be real cowhands!

Mr. Henderson nodded. "The desert is like no other place in the world. It has a stark beauty all its own."

"I can't wait to see it!" said the reverend.

"Oh, I'm afraid you'll have to wait, at least a little bit," said Mrs. Henderson with a smile. "Tomorrow you get to stay right here and help prepare breakfast and lunch. We have a lot of mouths to feed at our dude ranch!"

The reverend's face fell, and everyone

laughed—everyone except Luke. He dropped his fork on his plate with a loud *clink!*

The laughter quieted. Mrs. Henderson frowned at her son.

"May I be excused?" Luke asked. His voice was strained.

The Hendersons glanced at each other. Mrs. Henderson looked tired. She nodded at her husband.

"All right, son," said Mr. Henderson.

Luke immediately got up and left the room without a word.

Mr. Henderson called after him. "I'll expect to see you later at the campfire!"

Then there was silence. Mr. Henderson shook his head. "I'm sorry about that," he said. "Luke has been having a tough time adjusting to the idea of opening the ranch to strangers."

The reverend looked at the Hendersons with compassion. "It's quite all right," he said.

Mrs. Camden nodded. "You don't owe us any apologies."

Mrs. Henderson shook her head. "That isn't true. Luke's been acting very rudely, and I've grown impatient with him."

Lucy spoke up. "Mr. Henderson, Mrs.

Henderson . . . can I ask . . . what happened to his hand? Is that part of why he's so angry?"

"Lucy!" Mrs. Camden scolded. "I'm surprised at you. That isn't our business!"

"No, it's okay," Mr. Henderson said. "We should talk more about it. Then maybe things wouldn't be so . . . difficult."

"It happened four years ago," Mrs. Henderson said. "It was the summer after Luke's eighth-grade year. That was a good time for him. He was a success at school and at the rodeos."

Mrs. Henderson paused, then said, "Perhaps he was becoming proud."

"*I* was certainly proud of him," Mr. Henderson said.

"It was just like any other day," Mrs. Henderson continued. "Luke was out with the other hands, baling hay."

"Just like we do every year," said Mr. Henderson. "But this time, this one day, somehow Luke got his hand caught in the hay baler." Mrs. Henderson cringed. Mr. Henderson shook his head. "I was at the barn, and he was with the hands in the field. Even at that distance, I could hear him screaming."

"It was awful," Mrs. Henderson said. "I heard it, too, and came running out of the house."

Mr. Henderson nodded. "The boys brought him in on one of the trucks. By the time they got to us, Luke had passed out from the pain. We wrapped his hand and raced straight to the hospital in town."

"That was the longest ride of my life," said Mrs. Henderson. "I thought we'd never get there."

"But we did," said Mr. Henderson. "They fixed him up as best they could, but you saw his hand. The damage was pretty severe."

"I'm so sorry," said Mrs. Camden.

"Did Luke have a difficult time adjusting?" the reverend wanted to know.

Mr. Henderson nodded. "He dropped out of school. He just couldn't take people staring at him. So we asked a friend of ours who lives in the area, a retired teacher, to homeschool him."

Mrs. Henderson spoke up. "It was his pride, I'm realizing now." She looked at her husband. "We should have forced him to go back to school."

Mr. Henderson raised his hands helplessly. "How could we?"

"That's what would have been best for him," Mrs. Henderson insisted.

"At any rate," said Mr. Henderson, "he sticks pretty close to the ranch now. The people who work here all know him and are used to . . . his hand being the way it is. He isn't self-conscious around them. But when we told him we had to make the place into a dude ranch . . ."

Mrs. Henderson shook her head. "He didn't like the idea very much, that's for sure."

Lucy spoke up, suddenly understanding. "All those strangers coming here and staring at his hand, making him feel like a freak."

Mrs. Henderson nodded. "It will be very difficult for him."

"He's also very prideful about the ranch," said Mr. Henderson. "I think he feels ashamed that we have to open the ranch to tourists."

"If you'd like," said the reverend, "I could speak to Luke. As a minister, I counsel people with all sorts of different problems. Maybe I could help."

"Thank you, Reverend Camden," said Mr. Henderson. "I appreciate the offer. I doubt that Luke would agree to talk to you about it, but I'll let him know."

The reverend nodded.

"You know what's funny?" said Mrs. Henderson. "He's a better rider and roper now than he ever was, don't you agree, Cal?"

Mr. Henderson nodded. "That I do. It's amazing how he manages." He smiled at the Camdens. "I'm still so proud of him, you see."

After dinner they all helped clean up, then went out behind the house, where there was a fire circle. Before too long they had a nice-sized blaze going. While bats flitted back and forth in the darkness, Mr. Henderson told everyone a story about a prospector who'd gotten lost in the tunnels of his gold mines.

"He haunts that mine to this day," Mr. Henderson said. "Sometimes you can hear him moaning, still trying to find his way out."

They all shivered and stared up at the sky. The stars shone incredibly bright and sharp in the cool night air. The fire crackled and danced. Then into the silence came the sound of a long, low wail.

The hair on the back of Lucy's neck stood up. *Coyote,* Lucy thought. *That's just a coyote, right?*

The howl rose into the air again.

"What was that?" the reverend asked a little breathlessly.

Mr. Henderson poked at the fire with a stick. "Probably a lone wolf howling at the moon," he said.

Mr. Henderson's story had reminded Simon of his discovery in the den. After a moment, he cleared his throat and told everyone about it.

Mrs. Henderson spoke up. "That's very exciting!" she said. "I wonder who Beatrice's aunt was."

"Actually, Simon," said Mr. Henderson, "there *is* a formation of rocks near here called Rattlesnake Rock."

"Really?" Simon asked, his pulse quickening.

Mr. Henderson nodded. "Been called that for as long as I can remember."

Mrs. Henderson nodded. "Yep. That's what we called it when I was a little girl. It's called Rattlesnake Rock because it looks a little like a coiled rattler with his rattle sticking up in the air. Doesn't hurt that rattlesnakes seem to like to sleep there. They get out of the sun in the daytime, under the rocks."

"Tell you what," said Mr. Henderson. "Cody can take you out there tomorrow afternoon. He likes poking around there anyway, looking at the rattlers."

"Isn't that dangerous?" Mrs. Camden wanted to know.

Mr. Henderson shook his head. "He knows what he's doing. Right, Cody?"

Cody nodded at Mrs. Camden. "Yes, ma'am. I'm real careful. So long as you respect the snakes, they respect you."

Mrs. Camden looked doubtfully at Simon. "You be careful," she said.

"I will, Mom," Simon said.

They ended the evening with a song from Cody. He sang an old cowboy song in a surprisingly rich tenor.

When he was done, Mr. Henderson encouraged the Camdens to get some sleep. "Promises to be a long day tomorrow!" he said.

"Thank you for a lovely day," said Mrs.

Camden. They all thanked the Hendersons, then doused the fire.

As they walked back to the house, Lucy noticed that one of the downstairs bedroom lights was on. She thought she could hear the sound of a guitar being played softly. She thought of Luke sitting alone in his room and was sad. She'd come here to help a family keep its home, but one member of that family didn't want her help. In fact, the work that she was doing, even just her presence here, was painful to him.

Lucy went to sleep that night feeling more unsure of herself than she had in a long, long time.

SIX

Luke had told the truth. Days on the ranch did begin early, in the gray light just before dawn.

Mrs. Henderson bustled around, waking everyone up. She apologized with promises of hot coffee and a hearty breakfast. Downstairs, Mr. Henderson was waiting for them, bright-eyed and smiling.

"Luke and Cody are already outside, getting started. You folks take your time, eat your fill, then come on out and help."

"Not you, Reverend!" said Mrs. Henderson. "You have an appointment with me this morning!"

The reverend groaned and followed Mrs. Henderson into the kitchen.

After they'd eaten breakfast—scrambled eggs, hash browns, and bacon—they wandered outside. The air was surprisingly chill.

"The desert gets cold at night," Mrs. Camden said.

"It's weird, considering how hot it is in the daytime," said Lucy.

They were quiet as they gazed at the sun, just peeking over the rocky horizon.

A small group of volunteers was huddled together on the other side of the yard, talking in low voices and sipping coffee. Mrs. Camden recognized some of the people she'd worked with the day before. "I'm going to join them," she said to Lucy. "You and Simon and Ruthie go ahead and help with the horses and cattle."

"Oh, sure," said Simon. "Just leave us with the dirty work."

Mrs. Camden grinned. "There are some privileges that come with being a mom." The kids watched as their mom moseyed over to the group and poured herself a cup of coffee.

"Now what?" Ruthie asked.

Simon shrugged. "I guess we find Cody and Luke."

The question is, Lucy thought, *does Luke want to be found?*

Ruthie piped up, "I like Luke. He likes horses, and horses like him back."

Lucy smiled. "Speaking of horses," she said, "I'll bet the boys are in the stable."

When they got there, Luke was helping Cody pour oats into the horses' troughs. Lucy was struck again by the angular lines of Luke's brooding face. She also realized that after their encounter last night at the corral, she was more than a little nervous to talk to this unpredictable and moody guy.

"Hey, guys," Simon said as they walked up. "Can we help?"

Luke glanced at his wristwatch. "So you decided to show up, huh? Real ranchers get to work before the sun rises." He nodded at his brother. "Cody and I have been at it for an hour already. But I forgot. You're not real ranchers, are you? You're just on *vacation.*"

Ouch, Lucy thought. But what she said was, "I'm sorry. Your father didn't say anything about hurrying."

"Of course not," said Luke. "You're his guests. He's *pampering* you."

Luke turned to his brother. "Cody, can

you finish up here?" Cody nodded.

Luke turned back to the Camdens. "I'm going to the barn to help my dad load up the hay truck. It's hard work, but then again, that's what you're here for, right? The *dude* ranch experience?" Luke turned and walked out of the stable.

"*Man,*" Ruthie said under her breath. "*Somebody* woke up on the wrong side of the bed this morning."

"Is there anything we can do to help you, Cody?" Simon asked the boy.

"Naw, I got it," Cody said. Resting the bag of oats on his toe, he walked it across the passageway and set it against the wall. "If you want, you can come with me to the barn," Cody said as he led the way.

Simon and Lucy looked at each other. "Do we have a choice?" Simon asked.

Lucy shook her head. "I don't think so. Not if we want to be able to hold our heads up around here."

They followed Cody out of the stable and across the yard to the large barn on the other side of the corral. One entire side had been freshly painted.

"I'd rather be painting again," Simon muttered.

Lucy shrugged. "You can, if you want," she said.

"And leave you to face Luke alone? No way."

Lucy smiled her thanks.

Cody led them up to the loft of the barn, where there were huge stacks of hay bales. Luke was already hard at work, tossing bale after bale over the side of the loft. Parked below was a huge pickup truck. Mr. Henderson was standing in the truck's bed, stacking bales of hay as Luke tossed them down.

"Good morning, Camdens!" he called. "How was breakfast?"

"Good," said Simon. "Even considering that my dad helped to make it."

As Mr. Henderson laughed, Lucy couldn't help stealing a glance at Luke. He was concentrating on his work, balancing a hay bale against his hips and walking it across the floor. The muscles in his upper arms stood out sharply through the sleeves of his T-shirt. Apparently, his missing fingers didn't prevent him from doing chores.

Lucy watched as Luke tossed the bale over the side of the loft to his father in the truck below. Mr. Henderson knocked the bale to the floor of the truck bed, then hoisted it up and stacked it neatly behind him.

"Ruthie?" Mr. Henderson called. "Why don't you and Cody come down here and help me stack the bales. Simon and Lucy, you can help Luke."

"Later!" Ruthie said. She grabbed Cody's hand. "Come on!"

They ran to a ladder and started down to the floor.

Luke paused in his work to point to a wooden box built into the wall of the loft. Lucy noticed that he was wearing heavy leather work gloves. She glanced away, but not quickly enough to avoid seeing how most of the glove's fingers dangled empty.

"Get yourselves some gloves," Luke said.

"Come on," Lucy said to Simon. They walked over to the box and swung open the lid. Inside were about a dozen pairs of heavy work gloves. Lucy and Simon picked out a pair each and slid them on. They had a gritty, dirty feel. From working construction, Lucy was used to wearing gloves that other people had sweated in day after day. But Simon wasn't.

"These are really disgusting," he said quietly.

"Believe me," whispered Lucy, "you'll be glad you have them."

They walked back over to Luke. He didn't pause in his work. "Just grab a bale and drop it over the side," he said.

Lucy had thought the job would be easy, but the hay bales were much heavier than they looked! No wonder Luke was so strong. He'd been doing this every day since he'd been old enough to help.

Worse than the weight, though, was the wire that held the bales together. Even with the gloves, it cut into Lucy's hands. She was sure they would be red and chafed that night. But this was what Luke and Mr. Henderson did every day, and Lucy and Simon intended to help, even if they *were* just on vacation.

As they worked, Lucy sneaked glances at Luke when she could. Serious, concentrating on what he was doing, he was very attractive. It didn't hurt that his T-shirt clung to his powerful arms and chest.

Once, Lucy stumbled and brushed into

Luke, who was walking back to get another bale of hay. He reached out to steady her. Lucy looked up at him to smile her thanks, but Luke's eyes were as cold as stone.

After a few more minutes, Mr. Henderson called up to Lucy and Simon to take a break. "You're not used to the work!" he said. "Don't push it too hard the first day."

Feeling a little guilty, but grateful, Lucy and Simon leaned back against the wall, breathing hard and sweating.

She watched Luke. He hadn't looked at them or said anything, but Lucy could imagine the contempt he was feeling for them at that moment.

"This is hard work," Simon said, panting, "but I like it."

"Me too," Lucy said. "It feels good."

Simon nodded, and they got back to it.

The three of them worked without talking for a while longer. When Mr. Henderson finally called up to say that the truck was full, Lucy was glad. She needed a longer rest.

They climbed down the ladder. Mr. Henderson had already started up the truck. Ruthie and Cody were nowhere to be seen.

"Where'd the kids go?" Simon asked.

From the cab of the truck, Mr. Henderson answered, "I sent them off to play. They were throwing more hay than they were stacking!"

"I hope Ruthie wasn't a distraction for Cody," Lucy said worriedly.

"Oh, no," Mr. Henderson said. "I'm glad Ruthie's here. The summers can be lonely on the ranch. It's important for Cody to spend time with someone his age. Much more important than whatever work he might not be doing."

"Come on, Simon," Luke called from the bed of the truck. "You ride back here with me. *Ladies* get to ride up front."

Lucy looked sharply at Luke. The way he'd said *ladies* . . . Was he teasing her, or did he intend to be mean? Luke returned her look, but his gaze was blank.

While Simon climbed up next to Luke, Lucy walked around the front of the truck and got in next to Mr. Henderson.

The drive out to the north pasture would take a while. Mr. Henderson whistled softly as he drove. Lucy leaned back and peered out at the scenery as they bounced along. The grassy prairie gave way to massive outcrops of red rock, surrounded by huge boulders. The sun was still very low in the sky and lit the landscape dramatically. Lucy had never seen so many different kinds of cacti and desert flowers. Tired in her body and peaceful in her mind, Lucy drifted off to sleep.

SEVEN

The soft squeal of the truck's brakes woke Lucy from her catnap. She opened her eyes. Through the windshield she could see that the landscape had changed back to grassy prairie. Scattered across it was the Hendersons' vast herd of cattle.

Lucy glanced over at Mr. Henderson. He was sitting with one hand resting on the steering wheel. On his face was a look of utter contentment. "There they are," he said, almost in a whisper.

At Mr. Henderson's direction, Lucy hopped down out of the cab and up into the bed of the truck. Luke explained that his father would now drive the truck through the herd. It was their job to push out the hay bales.

The truck dropped into gear and began to move. Luke reached down and un-latched the gate on the back of the truck. Then he started kicking bales out. They dropped to the ground and broke apart. The cattle nearby lowed and, heads bobbing, started to graze.

The three of them worked together silently. Simon moved bales from the front and stacked them in the middle of the truck bed. Lucy hoisted them from there to Luke at the gate, who pushed them out. Lucy got into a rhythm, enjoying herself and momentarily forgetting about what was going on with Luke. She was only aware of their working together as a team, from Simon to her to Luke.

Lucy was surprised when all the hay bales were gone in what seemed like a short time. There was hay scattered about the bed of the truck, but no bales. She looked at Simon, who was stretching. She looked over at Luke. He pushed the last bale off the back. Then he stood and squinted out over the cattle.

Lucy couldn't see his face, but something about the way Luke stood there reminded her of his father when they'd first arrived at the pasture, the grin on his face as he had looked over the herd.

Luke loves this place just as much as his father does, Lucy realized.

The drive back to the house took much longer than Lucy expected. This time she rode in the back of the truck with the boys. They were all quiet, resting. Simon dozed off, leaving Lucy and Luke to bob along in silence.

The sun had climbed higher in the sky while they'd worked, and the air was heating up fast. Without giving herself time to think, Lucy blurted out, "It's getting hot."

Luke seemed to stiffen. He hesitated, as if mulling over his response to her simple comment, and then answered, "Yep."

Nice one, Luce, Lucy thought. *Way to break the ice.*

They rode on in silence until Luke suddenly said, "There's a swimming hole."

"What?" Lucy asked.

Luke cleared his throat. "A swimming hole. There's one near the house. If you're hot, you can go swimming before lunch."

"Oh," Lucy said. "Thanks."

They were quiet again, and Lucy wondered, *What's going on? Is he actually being friendly?*

When they got back to the house, Lucy and Simon quickly changed into their swimsuits and followed Luke out to a natural pond at the bottom of a small, rocky ravine. Ruthie and Cody were already there, splashing around and laughing.

"Come on in!" Ruthie called when she saw her brother and sister. "The water's great!"

Simon waded in. The bottom of the pond was smooth and sandy. Lucy walked in up to her waist and dove from there. The water was surprisingly clear and refreshingly cool.

Lucy floated on her back and relaxed while Simon swam laps. Luke stood on the bank and watched them. The way the shadows were falling, Lucy couldn't see his face. He was just a dark silhouette on the rocks.

Why isn't he coming swimming with us? Lucy wondered.

At the other end of the pond, Ruthie and Cody whooped and hollered boisterously. Their voices echoed oddly in the ravine, somehow emphasizing the vastness of the desert around them and the blue sky above.

Cody shouted for Luke to join them. Lucy watched as Luke stood silent for a moment more, then turned and walked away.

For lunch their dad and Mrs. Henderson had prepared tacos. It was a rowdy affair. There weren't enough seats around the table to accommodate all the hands, so Lucy ended up having her tacos out on the porch with her mom.

Mrs. Camden was tired and dirty from her morning's work, but clearly happy. She smiled at her daughter. "Are you having a good time?"

Lucy thought about it a moment. "I guess I'd say I'm having an *interesting* time."

"*Mmmm . . . ,*" Mrs. Camden said, her mouth full of taco. "What does that mean?"

"I mean, it's beautiful here," Lucy

explained. "And it feels really good to be helping the Hendersons. . . ."

"But . . . ?" her mother asked.

"I guess I'm confused about Luke," Lucy admitted.

Mrs. Camden grew serious. "Yes, well, I can understand that. I was so angry at myself yesterday when I embarrassed him."

"But *you* didn't embarrass him, Mom! That's just the point!"

"What do you mean?" asked Mrs. Camden.

"How could you have known about his hand?" Lucy said. "He made *you* feel embarrassed when he made such a big deal about it."

Mrs. Camden considered Lucy's comment. "So you think it's *not* a big deal?" she asked.

Lucy frowned. "No, of course not." She shook her head. "I guess I don't know what I mean. Socially, maybe it's only as big a deal as he lets it be."

They were quiet for a moment, munching on their tacos. They watched a group of volunteers across the yard working on the engine of a truck.

"He doesn't want us here," Lucy said abruptly.

"Who?" her mother asked. "Luke?"

Lucy nodded. "He doesn't want to open the ranch to tourists. He doesn't want our help."

"What he wants isn't really the issue," Mrs. Camden said. "His parents have decided that it's the best way to save their home."

"I know," Lucy said. She was confused. Every time she'd felt uncertain about herself in the past, she'd been able to throw herself into some kind of work that helped other people. She had always been able to count on that to help her find herself again. But this time . . . Certainly, Luke's parents appreciated what Lucy and her family were doing. But did that mean Lucy should just ignore Luke? What she was *helping* them to do was *hurting* him.

Mrs. Camden broke the silence. "Do you remember last night at dinner when Mrs. Henderson said that she and Mr. Henderson should have made Luke go back to school?"

Lucy nodded.

"That would have been unpleasant for

Luke. Obviously, it was something Luke didn't want. But it might have been better for him."

"You think what we're doing is the same thing?"

Mrs. Camden shrugged. "I don't know. I think it's difficult to know what's best for other people. It's hard enough to do that for yourself."

"But . . . ?" Lucy prodded.

Mrs. Camden smiled. "*But,* I can't help feeling that Mrs. Henderson was right. It's wrong for Luke to hide himself away because of his hand. I don't think that can be good for him—or for anybody, for that matter. How long can he avoid new people? It's already been four years. Would it be good for him to live his whole life like that?"

Lucy shook her head. "Of course not. At least, *in theory.*"

"Right," said her mom. "It's easy to talk about it, to think you know what's best. But it's another thing entirely to actually have to live it."

Lucy sighed. "So what can I do?"

"About Luke? That's hard. Maybe all you can do is to be there for him."

"Looking at his hand," Lucy said.

Her mom nodded. "That's right. Whether you know it or not—whether Luke wants it or not—you're giving him an opportunity to face something. The hard part is, you can't help him do it. That's up to Luke, all by himself."

After lunch, Cody took Ruthie and Simon out to Rattlesnake Rock. It was some distance from the house, so they decided to ride. Cody saddled up Dusty, and Ruthie a pony named Desert Star. Simon—not the most accomplished rider—was given a gentle gelding named Roebuck.

"Come on, Simon!" Ruthie teased. "There's nothing to it!"

Simon sat atop his horse uncomfortably. "You're sure he won't run off with me or something?" he asked Shelly, the horse wrangler, who'd helped him put on Roebuck's saddle and bridle.

Shelly smiled up at Simon reassuringly. "He's the gentlest horse in the stable. You might even have some trouble getting him to move!"

Ruthie laughed, and Cody hid a smile

behind his hand, but that sounded perfectly all right to Simon. As they rode out across the grassland, Simon couldn't quite shake the feeling that he was slowly sliding off Roebuck's back.

Not cool, he thought.

Ruthie and Cody cantered off on a race or two, but never out of Simon's sight. And they always came back.

Before too long, the three of them left the prairie behind and entered an area where the ground was dry and rocky. Desert flowers and cacti grew all around, and lizard after lizard zipped in and out of the rocks.

Cody rode up beside Simon. "There it is," he said, pointing off to the right.

Simon looked and saw a jumble of rocks. As they rode closer, Simon could begin to see why the formation was called Rattlesnake Rock. It really did look like a coiled rattler!

"Cool," Simon said.

They dismounted. That is, Ruthie and Cody dismounted. When Simon tried to swing his leg over the back of the horse, he got caught, half on and half off. Roebuck looked back at him with one big eye.

"What are *you* looking at?" Simon asked. Grunting, he managed to free his leg and tumble down off the horse, landing on his rear. He got up and brushed off his jeans.

Roebuck snorted dismissively and started to graze. Simon hurried to catch up to Ruthie and Cody. Before leaving the ranch, they'd all put on cowboy boots— Cody had an old pair that fit Ruthie, and Simon was wearing an old pair of Mr. Henderson's. The boots would provide some protection from sharp fangs, should one of them stumble upon a rattlesnake and surprise it. And they all wore cowboy hats to protect their faces from the sun.

Cody also carried a flashlight and a long stick. Simon didn't particularly want to know what the stick was for.

"What did the letter say again?" Ruthie asked.

"Not much," Simon admitted. "It just said to begin the search here, at Rattlesnake Rock."

The kids looked over the rock formation. It didn't cover that much ground, but they didn't even know what they were looking for.

They began to wander through the rocks, carefully looking into crevices and flipping over small stones with their feet. The sun beat down on them and glared painfully off the rocks and into their eyes.

"Keep your ears open," Cody warned them. "A rattlesnake will try to let you know it's there by shaking its rattle."

Simon climbed up on one of the bigger rocks and looked around. Not having any better ideas, he climbed over to the rattle part of the formation and stood next to it. This close, the red rock towered over him by several feet. Simon was walking around it, wondering if something could have been left on top, when he heard the spine-tingling shake of a rattle.

Simon froze. He opened his mouth to call out, but no sound would come. He tried again. "Ruthie!" he croaked.

But when he turned ever so slowly to look for his little sister, he saw that she too was frozen, just feet behind him.

"There . . . ," Ruthie whispered, cautiously lifting a hand and pointing to a dark space under the rattle rock. "I can see something moving in there!"

Carefully, Simon backed away, and the rattling sound subsided. Simon was breathing a little easier when Cody climbed up next to him.

Cody squatted down at a safe distance and beamed his flashlight into the darkness. "Yep," he said. "That's a rattler, all right."

"Well?" Ruthie said. "How are we going to get him out?"

"You want to get him out?" Simon asked incredulously.

"Of course!" Ruthie said. "Don't you want to see him?"

"Not particularly," Simon admitted.

Cody was still staring into the crevice. "I think there's something else in there," he said.

"What?" Simon asked.

Cody shook his head. "I don't know, but I think I can see *something* near the rattler's coils."

Simon bent down to look, ready to jump away at the least sign of movement. In the flashlight's beam he could see the snake, its round body and shining eyes. And . . . was Cody right? Was there something else glinting in there?

"How do we get to it?" Simon asked.

Cody held up a stick as long as Simon was tall. "Do you want to try?"

"Uh . . . no, not really."

Cody shrugged. Very carefully, he extended the stick into the crevice. The sound of the rattler got louder and louder.

The rattler struck in Cody's direction, trying to slither its way up the stick. As Cody drew the stick out of the hole, he maneuvered it so that the twisting, slithering snake was far from his body—and the Camdens!—at all times. Finally, Cody flung the snake over the side of the rock with a triumphant grin.

"*Whew!* Nice job!" Simon said.

Cody smiled. "Thanks," he said. "That one was quick."

The three of them gathered around the crevice, and Cody beamed the flashlight back into the darkness.

"A box?" Ruthie said.

"I can't tell," said Simon. He looked carefully to make sure there wasn't another snake hiding under there, then used another stick to push the object out.

"It *is* a box," Simon said as the object emerged. It was a shallow tin box, covered with dust.

"*Cool,*" Ruthie crooned.

"Open it," Cody breathed.

The box seemed to be sealed tight, but Simon found a catch and slid it to the side. The top of the box popped open slightly, and Simon lifted the lid.

Inside was a letter. Simon immediately recognized the writing. "It's another note from Beatrice's aunt!"

Carefully, Simon lifted the note out of the box and opened it. It read:

Congratulations, Beatrice!

I knew you'd find my letter. How many hours did we spend here? You playing among the rocks while I painted the sky?

There's another place where we used to spend time. Do you remember? We called it the stream of green. That is where you must go next if you hope to find our treasure.

All my love,

Your doting Aunt

"Wow," Ruthie said.

Simon looked at Cody. "Do you know what the stream of green is?" Simon asked. Cody shook his head. "That's okay. Maybe someone back at the house does."

Simon looked up. The sun was dropping lower in the sky, and the light was getting yellowish. It would soon be time for dinner.

"Let's get back," Simon said. He was excited. It was hard to believe, but he was on a real treasure hunt!

EIGHT

At dinner that night, Simon asked about the stream of green, but neither Mr. nor Mrs. Henderson knew what it referred to.

"You might want to check with some of our cowhands when we go on the drive," Mr. Henderson said. "They might have an idea."

"Speaking of the cattle drive . . . ," Reverend Camden said.

Mr. Henderson laughed. "For a greenhorn, you're certainly eager, Reverend!"

Mrs. Camden grinned. "It's been his lifelong dream to be a cowboy."

"I hate to disappoint you, Reverend," Mr. Henderson said, "but we need to delay the drive a day. One of the trucks we use to get out to the herd isn't working."

"I thought we'd ride horses out to the herd," the reverend said.

"That's how they did it in the old days," said Mrs. Henderson. "Nowadays we use trucks to get out there. Saves us half a day. We bring the horses with us and use them on the way back."

As they ate and talked, Lucy kept her eye on Luke. He behaved much the way he had the night before, keeping his head down and staying quiet. Once again, Lucy was feeling uncomfortably ineffective. Just this afternoon she'd been feeling great, using her skills to do needed work, ripping up the floor in the back of the house. She was part of a team, contributing to something larger than herself. But now, looking at Luke sitting across the table, she questioned that feeling. How had her accomplishments today helped him? If he didn't want her help, what was the point?

After dinner they retired to the campfire. Luke came with them this time and brought his guitar. While his father told stories, Luke strummed along quietly.

How can he play so well with missing fingers? Lucy wondered. She cringed at the insensitivity of the thought. But as she mulled it over, she remembered her talk with her mother that afternoon. Anyone who knew about Luke's hand would wonder the same thing. It was totally normal. If her mother was right, Lucy would be doing Luke a service by *not* shielding him from it.

Still, that night when she got into bed, Lucy set her alarm to get up even earlier than she had that morning. When Luke got to work, Lucy intended to be there waiting for him.

Maybe it was something about the clean air at the ranch or the hard work she'd taken part in the day before. Whatever it was, Lucy slept soundly and woke up a minute before her alarm was set to go off. It was pitch-black, but Lucy sprang out of bed, refreshed.

When she showed up in the dining room, Mr. Henderson was sitting at the table, drinking coffee and looking over some papers.

"Well!" he said when he saw Lucy. "Looks like we got ourselves a real rancher here!"

Lucy beamed with pleasure. When

Luke stepped out of the kitchen, a cup of coffee in his hand, he looked shocked.

"What do you think you're doing?" he asked.

Lucy gave him a smug smile. She considered it a victory to have gotten a reaction out of him.

"Going to work," she said casually.

"Come on in here, honey!" called Mrs. Henderson from the kitchen.

Lucy stepped around Luke and walked into the kitchen. Even at this early hour, it seemed a busy place, steamy and full of good smells. "Can I get you a cup of coffee?" Mrs. Henderson asked.

"No, thanks," Lucy said. "But I'd welcome a tall glass of orange juice."

"Luke, pour this girl a glass of orange juice!" Mrs. Henderson commanded.

Grumbling, Luke put down his coffee and went to the refrigerator to get the juice.

"It's awfully nice to be up so early," Lucy said.

"Doesn't seem early to me," Luke retorted under his breath.

Lucy ignored him. "The whole day ahead of you . . ."

"That's right!" Mr. Henderson called from the living room.

Luke poured Lucy a glass of OJ and handed it to her.

"Thanks," she said.

"You're welcome," said Luke.

Lucy scrutinized Luke's face. Was it just her imagination, or had Luke actually sounded grudgingly nice there for a moment?

But his face betrayed nothing. It was as emotionless as ever.

Cody came downstairs shortly after, and the three of them went out to feed the horses. Lucy enjoyed spending a little time with each animal. She could understand why Ruthie liked these big, elegant beasts.

Ruthie and Simon soon joined them, and they went to the barn to load the hay the way they had the day before. Then they drove out to the herd and fed them. By the time they got back, Mrs. Henderson was ringing the bell for lunch.

When she got to the dining room, Lucy looked around for Luke. The room was crowded, but he didn't seem to be there. Lucy poked her head into the kitchen. Her dad had on a KISS ME, I COOK apron and was making sandwiches.

"Hey, Dad," Lucy said. "Have you seen Luke around?"

"He was just here," the reverend answered. "He grabbed a sandwich to go. Said he had work to do and wanted to get an early start on the afternoon."

"Thanks, Dad!" Lucy said. She grabbed a sandwich for herself and ran back out toward the front of the house. Something told Lucy that she was making headway with Luke. She didn't want to let him get away from her!

She ran out the screen door and saw Luke walking toward the barn.

"Hey!" Lucy called.

Luke hesitated, and Lucy hurried down the porch steps and across the yard.

"Where are you off to?" she asked when she'd caught up to him.

"There's some fence that needs mending. I thought I'd slip away and get to work on that."

Lucy nodded. She fell into step beside him. "Want some help?" she asked, and took a bite of her sandwich.

Luke shrugged. "It's really just a one-person job. . . ."

"Oh," Lucy said. They walked together past the stable to the barn. Suddenly Luke paused. He seemed to be looking everywhere but at Lucy.

Playing a hunch, Lucy said, "Why don't I come along anyway? I'd enjoy a drive."

For a moment, Lucy thought Luke would say no. Then his eyes stilled.

"Suit yourself," he said.

Parked in the barn was the pickup truck. Luke walked around and got into the cab. Lucy climbed up beside him.

He started the truck and pulled out of the barn. He drove surely, with the same look of concentration and intensity on his face that she'd observed when they were loading the hay. There was something about that expression—the determination or intelligence, she wasn't sure—but Lucy found it very attractive.

Luke didn't say anything as they drove over a dirt road and out into the grassland surrounding the ranch. Lucy was quiet herself, just being with him. She rolled down her window and let the hot wind blow in.

She closed her eyes and faced into it. It brushed softly against her face and lifted her hair. Lucy wondered if Luke was watching her but didn't turn to see.

"There's something I wanted to ask you," Lucy said suddenly, surprising herself. She was nervous, but something told her this was a good time.

Lucy turned from the wind to look at Luke. He didn't take his eyes from the road as the truck jolted and bounced over bumps.

"What?" he finally asked.

Lucy turned away again. "Your guitar playing last night was beautiful. I was wondering, did you play before your accident? Or was it something you learned to do afterwards?"

Beside her, Luke was silent. She felt quiet emanating from him, as if he was holding himself very still.

Lucy resisted the urge to turn and look at him. Instead, she affected nonchalance, watching the land slip by outside her window.

She heard him draw a breath. In a choked voice, he said, "After."

Now Lucy looked at him. He appeared the same as before, both hands on the wheel and eyes glued to the road. But Lucy had the distinct impression that he was trembling.

"Was it hard?" Lucy asked softly.

Luke jerked a stiff nod. "Yeah," he said.

Lucy nodded, as if this were the most normal conversation in the world. She turned back to the windshield and stared out at the road with him, not sure what else to say.

They traveled in silence for a while, then Luke said, "I had to see if I could do it. I *had* to do it."

"You play beautifully," Lucy said.

Luke smiled and glanced down, as if embarrassed. In that moment his face and his smile were perfectly sweet.

"Thank you," Luke said. "I can't really fingerpick so well, since, you know . . ."

Lucy nodded.

"So I mostly use a pick. That isn't any problem at all. You just need your thumb and first finger for that."

They rode on in companionable silence. Running along the road was a fence made of wire strung between wooden posts.

"Is this the fence that we need to mend?" Lucy asked.

Luke nodded. "It's just up ahead here."

Luke pulled up next to a section of the fence where the barbed wires had come away from the posts. "Here we are," he said.

"If the cows never go through this," Lucy asked, "how'd the fence get pulled down?"

"High winds," Luke explained. He turned off the truck and got out.

Duh, Lucy thought. She opened her door and walked back to the bed of the truck. Luke had opened the tailgate and was pulling out a toolbox, two pairs of work gloves, and a roll of barbed wire.

"Here," he said, holding out one pair of gloves to Lucy. When Lucy took them from him, she imagined brushing her hand against his, but didn't. The way he was holding his hand, Lucy couldn't tell there was anything wrong with it.

They walked to the fence and found the last post where the wire was still attached. Luke cut the bad wire off. Then he took the end of the spool, attached it to the post, and, unrolling as he went, walked to the next post, where he attached the wire. He did the same at the next post, and so on, until he reached a post where the original wire was still attached.

"That's all there is to it," Luke said. "I told you, a one-man job."

"Can I do the bottom wire?" Lucy asked.

"Sure," Luke said. He handed her the roll of wire, and Lucy duplicated what Luke had just done, but for the lowest wire of the fence.

When she'd clipped the replacement wire free of the roll and attached it to the final post, she turned to get Luke's reaction.

He was standing with his arms crossed, watching her out of narrowed eyes.

"Well?" Lucy asked.

"Not bad," said Luke.

They went to the back of the truck and put the equipment away. When they got back into the cab, Lucy said, "Where now?"

"That isn't enough for you?" Luke asked.

Lucy shrugged. "It didn't take long. We're all the way out here. Is there anything else that needs to be done?"

Luke thought about it. Then he put the truck in gear.

"Well?" Lucy asked.

Luke just looked at her.

Lucy felt a shiver run down her spine. She really didn't know this guy at all. Who knew what he'd do?

You don't, she thought. *And that's why you like him.*

They drove for a while. It seemed to Lucy that they were heading back in the general direction of the ranch, but she didn't recognize the landscape. She leaned back and enjoyed the drive.

After a while, they approached a lightly wooded area. Luke parked at the edge of it and turned off the engine. He opened his door and started to get out but stopped when he saw that Lucy wasn't moving.

"Come on," he said. "I want to show you something."

Luke led Lucy through the chaparral. They went slowly over the uneven ground. At one point Lucy stumbled, and Luke reached out to steady her. It took a moment before they realized he'd reached out with his right hand. Luke immediately let go of her arm and put his hand in his pocket.

"Sorry," Luke said, embarrassed.

"It's okay," said Lucy. She was both excited by his touch and, she had to admit, a little repulsed. His thumb and first finger pinched around her bare arm had felt so strange. . . .

Before long they came to a clearing. In the middle of the clearing was what looked like the foundation of a sprawling house, surrounded by piles of stones. They walked into the clearing among the stones.

"What was this?" Lucy asked. "It looks so old."

"It is," Luke answered. "My mother's family lived here a long time ago, before they built the house we live in now."

Lucy touched a moss-covered rock. "You're lucky," Lucy said.

Luke raised his eyebrows. "Oh?"

Lucy smiled at what he wasn't saying— that a guy who'd been through what he had couldn't be *that* lucky.

"*Yes,*" Lucy said. "You're lucky to have so much of your family's history around you. It's no wonder that you and your parents are so connected to this land."

Luke placed the flat of his right hand against one of the stones and spread out the stumps of his fingers. He let out a breath and stared down at his hand.

Lucy shivered, but this time not from excitement or fear. "It's getting cold," she said. "Maybe we should go back."

Luke stirred and slipped his hand back into his pocket. "Okay," he said.

"Thanks for showing this to me," Lucy said.

Luke nodded but didn't look up. "Sure."

They walked to the truck and got in. On the drive back, Lucy had the distinct feeling that Luke was drawing away from her, that there was a sudden distance between them. That was all right with her. If he needed space, she'd give it to him.

Back at the ranch, dinner was still some time away, and the volunteers were still busy working. Luke parked the truck in the barn.

"See you at dinner?" Lucy asked.

"Sure," Luke answered, sounding a little surprised.

Lucy smiled at him and hopped out of the truck. *How's* that *for playing hard to get?* she thought smugly.

She spent the rest of the afternoon helping with the floor she'd worked on the day before. At the end of the day, she said goodbye to her volunteer friends as they headed home. The floor was almost finished. Their next project would be the stairs—and what a project that would be! But they'd have to wait to really get to work until the Camdens left, since their bedrooms were up there. Lucy was sorry that she was going to miss it.

After being around so many people during the day, dinner was a welcome change. As usual, it was just the Camdens and the Hendersons.

Mr. Henderson asked everyone about their day.

Simon went first. As he talked about painting the barn, Lucy threw a glance at Luke. She was glad to see that he seemed much less guarded than he'd been at previous dinners. He even laughed when Simon described having a bucket of white paint dumped over his head.

Lucy thought that Mrs. Henderson noticed the difference, too. At one point, she gave Lucy a long, thoughtful look.

Ruthie reported that she'd spent the day swimming and riding.

"Working hard," Simon teased.

"It *is* hard work!" Ruthie said seriously.

Mrs. Camden talked about the bunkhouses and how well they were coming along. "You'll be proud to have guests there," she said.

Lucy saw Luke flinch slightly when her mom said that. But he didn't retreat from the conversation. And when Lucy started talking about their progress on the floor, Luke watched her carefully.

He's wondering if I'll talk about what we did together, Lucy guessed. But she wasn't going to. It felt too . . . private.

"That's all well and good," Reverend Camden said when they'd all finished. "But what I want to know is, when are we going on that cattle drive?"

"I have to admit," Mrs. Camden said with a smile, "I'm getting pretty excited about riding the range myself."

Mr. Henderson laughed. "That'll be tomorrow."

Reverend Camden pumped his fist in Ruthie-like fashion. "Yes!"

"Usually, we'd take the trucks out to the herd, but we still can't seem to get one of them running. . . ." Mr. Henderson looked a little embarrassed.

"Does that mean we'll ride out?" Ruthie asked eagerly.

Mrs. Henderson nodded. "That's right, dear."

Now it was Ruthie's turn to pump her fist. "Yes!"

Simon groaned. "How long will it take?"

"Not long at all," Mr. Henderson said reassuringly. "Maybe four or five hours to get to the herd. Then another five or six to run them down to the south pasture."

Simon dropped his face into his hands. "I'm not going to make it!"

Lucy laughed. "Oh, the drama!"

Mrs. Henderson clapped her hands together. "Okay, that's enough chitchat! Everybody to bed!"

Luke looked surprised and, Lucy thought, maybe a little disappointed. "No campfire tonight, Mom?" he asked.

"Nope," she said, getting up and collecting plates. "Tomorrow's going to be a long day."

Lucy smiled as she stood up. At least she wouldn't be the *only* Camden waking up early tomorrow!

NINE

Morning came much too early for Simon. He groggily dragged himself down to breakfast, where the Hendersons were irritatingly chipper.

"Big ride today, Simon!" Mr. Henderson said, clapping him on the shoulder.

"Heh, heh. Yeah," Simon said half-heartedly. He collapsed at the dining room table and put his head in his hands. *Oh, brother!*

Except for Ruthie, the rest of the Camdens looked pretty much the way Simon felt.

Coming in and out of the house were men wearing leather riding chaps over their boots. Simon hadn't seen any of them before

and figured they just showed up for the cattle drives.

Breakfast helped to pep the Camdens
up a bit. After eating, they walked outside.
They could smell the smoke from the
woodstove in one of the bunkhouses. It
mixed with the rich smell of horses and
leather in the cool predawn air.

The reverend leaned back and patted
his stomach. "Now *this* is the life!"

In the yard in front of the house stood a
group of horses, most of them with riders.
Shelly paired Mrs. Camden and Lucy with
horses, since they hadn't ridden yet. As the
dough puncher, the reverend would be driv-
ing the chuck wagon.

Roebuck was waiting for Simon. The
horse seemed to be rolling its eyes at him.
"What?" Simon said. "Just be a nice horse."

Simon grabbed the saddle and put his
foot into the stirrup. Jumping a bit to get off
the ground, he heaved himself into the saddle. "There," he said, "that wasn't . . . hey!"
Roebuck's head and neck were missing! It
took Simon a moment to realize he was sitting backward, facing the horse's haunches!

"Nice move, Simon," Ruthie teased.
"You put the wrong foot in the stirrup!"

Grumbling, Simon slid down off Roebuck's back and tried again, this time careful to put his left foot in the stirrup. When he landed in the saddle, Roebuck's neck and head were right where they were supposed to be.

Simon gave the horse a pat on the neck. "See?" he said. "You're in good hands." Roebuck just snorted and shook his mane.

Somewhere near the front of the group, Mr. Henderson stood up in his stirrups and called, "Everybody ready? Let's go!"

Lucy stretched a little in the saddle and smiled. This was great! She was riding a pretty bay mare named Sunset, but it was the sunrise that occupied her attention. As the morning sun painted the desert, she was sure she saw wolves or coyotes—she didn't know which—slinking off to their dens in the distance.

Riding with the group were several cowboys who were there to help drive the cattle. Everyone was wearing boots, leather chaps, and cowboy hats. Some of the riders also wore light fleece vests that could be easily removed. Although it was chilly right now, it would be blazing hot soon enough.

Lucy looked at Luke, riding at the front

of the group with his father. She wondered what this day would bring, whether she'd get to spend any time with him. She hoped so. She was really starting to like him despite his surly attitude.

The group rode through the sunrise for several hours without incident. It was glorious as the sun peeked over a distant plateau, slowly staining the desert red again.

Late in the morning Lucy started to feel a little fidgety in the saddle. She wasn't used to sitting in one place for so long, especially when the place she was sitting in was moving!

They broke at about one o'clock to eat lunch and to let the heat of the day pass over them.

Lucy watched her mom dismount and noticed she was walking a little funny. When Lucy dismounted, she realized why. Her thighs and rear end hurt! *So this is what saddle sore means,* Lucy thought.

Gingerly, Lucy sat down, but that was even worse. She stood back up and tried to stretch. The grimace on Simon's face must have mirrored hers.

"How is it?" asked someone from behind her. Lucy spun around to find Luke smiling at her.

"How's *what*?" Lucy asked, feigning ignorance.

"You know," Luke said, raising his eyebrows and politely glancing down.

Lucy felt herself blush a little. "Oh, that. Um . . . a little uncomfortable?"

Luke smiled. "Riding for hour after hour *does* take some getting used to."

"Great," Lucy said.

Mrs. Camden walked over to them with obvious discomfort. "Howdy, Luke."

Luke touched the brim of his hat with the finger of his right hand. "Ma'am."

"This is just going to get worse, isn't it?" Mrs. Camden asked.

Luke smiled a bit, not unkindly. "I'm afraid so, Mrs. Camden."

Mrs. Camden shook her head. "I guess that's what we get for vacationing at a dude ranch!"

The smile froze on Luke's face, and Lucy caught her breath. Mrs. Camden immediately realized what had happened.

"I'm sorry, Luke," she said. "That was a thoughtless thing to say."

Looking like he had to force himself

to move, Luke reached up and tapped the brim of his hat again. "Not at all, ma'am," he said a little stiffly. "You ladies have a good lunch, now."

He turned and walked away.

Lucy glared at her mother. "Mom!"

Mrs. Camden raised her hands apologetically. "I'm sorry! He's just *so* sensitive."

Lucy watched Luke walk through the camp, exchanging greetings with the cowboys squatting on the ground. He walked easily among them, his hands tucked into his jeans pockets. There was something about the way he moved that was so right. . . .

This is his place, Lucy thought.

"Come and get it!" called the reverend from the chuck wagon. The cowboys jumped to their feet and hurried over. Knowing who the cook was, the Camdens moved a little more slowly.

The reverend was looking proud of himself, dishing out pinto beans with meat and bread. "There you are," he said to one cowboy. "Eat up!"

"Thanks, Cookie," the cowboy said.

When Lucy got to the front of the line, the reverend's face lit up. "Lucy! From my very own family. Here's a little extra, just because I like you."

"Gee, thanks," Lucy said, retreating to the camp and squatting down to eat. She grimaced with her first spoonful. Somehow her dad had managed to burn the beans!

She glanced around to take in the cowboys' reactions, but they seemed unperturbed. They were wolfing everything down as if they ate burned beans every day. *Maybe they do!* Lucy thought with a grin.

After lunch everyone saddled back up and rode on. If Lucy thought getting out of the saddle after riding for hours was hard, getting back in was torture!

It was late afternoon when they got to the herd. Mr. Henderson called everyone to come in around him.

"What we're going to do now," he said, "is round up the cattle and start for the south pasture. Each of our guests will pair up with a more experienced hand, ride out to the edges of the herd, and begin to drive them. I figure we've got . . ." Mr. Henderson squinted up at the sun. ". . . maybe a couple of hours before we break for the evening. Okay? Hands, please pair off with a guest."

Lucy immediately thought of Luke, but

he had sidled up next to his father and was talking something over. As she watched, their discussion became more and more heated.

"Miss?" someone said.

Lucy looked over her shoulder. An older man with white stubble on his chin was sitting on a horse slightly behind her.

"My name's Ben. Would you care to join me for the roundup?"

Lucy glanced over at Luke, but he and his father were still talking. *Arguing*, Lucy thought.

Lucy turned back to Ben and smiled. "I'd love to. Thank you, Ben."

"Not at all. You're Lucy, right?"

Lucy nodded.

"Do you have much experience riding?" Ben asked.

"Actually, no," Lucy admitted.

They talked about what they were going to do as they rode at a fast trot out to one edge of the herd. In the distance, Lucy could see other pairs taking their places.

"As you can see, we're encircling the herd," Ben explained. "We keep 'em moving and keep 'em together by making noise, like this: *Yippee!*"

The cows nearest them picked up their heads and started to move away. All along the edges of the herd, Lucy could hear the other cowhands calling, *"Yippee!"* Slowly, the herd began to move.

Ben urged his horse forward. *"Yippee! Yippee!"* he cried. He turned to Lucy. "You try it!"

Feeling a little foolish, Lucy said, "Yippee?"

"Like you mean it!" Ben said.

Lucy took a deep breath. *"Yippee!"* she cried.

Ben laughed. "That's the way! Now put some space between you and me so we can watch over more cows."

Lucy guided Sunset away from Ben. *"Yippee!"* she called to the cows right in front of her. They moved away, their heads bobbing.

"Keep 'em going in the right direction!" Ben called. *"Yippee!"*

Lucy smiled. As silly as it seemed, she felt responsible for the cows in her general vicinity. It was up to her to take care of them, and that was a nice feeling!

They drove the cattle for about two

hours before breaking for the day. There was only one moment of excitement before then. One of the cows broke from the herd, and the cowhand to go after it, pushing her horse to a gallop, was Ruthie!

"*Yaw!*" she cried. "*Yippee!*"

She got in front of the cow, stopped it, and guided it back to the herd.

That night, Ruthie was the toast of the camp! As the reverend served everyone their dinner of green beans and burgers, he kept repeating how that was *his* daughter.

Lucy kept her eyes peeled for Luke—she hadn't seen him all day. Now, as she listened to the cowhands swap stories, she saw him, hanging back from the circle in the shadows. Grimacing at her sore muscles, she got up to return her plate to the chuck wagon, then wandered over to stand beside Luke.

"Hey," Lucy said. Luke glanced at her, then turned his attention back to the fire. "How was your ride?" Lucy tried again.

"Same as it usually is," replied Luke.

Lucy nodded. "Right. Okay, I thought I'd just say hello." She started back toward the fire.

"Lucy, wait," Luke said.

Lucy paused and looked at him over her shoulder.

"My ride was fine. How was yours?"

Lucy stepped back beside him. "Fun! I rode with Ben. He taught me lots of interesting things, and I liked being responsible for the cattle."

Luke nodded. "Ben's a good hand," he said.

"I looked for you when we were pairing up, but you were . . . busy."

By the fire, Ruthie was delivering another blow-by-blow account of how she'd saved the wayward cow.

Luke grimaced. "My dad didn't warn me that you guests were actually going to be helping drive the cattle. It took me by surprise."

"We *guests*?" Lucy asked. She sighed. "You make it sound like a bad word."

"Maybe it is, to me."

"What about me?" Lucy asked. "Is that what I am to you, too? Just a bad word?"

"That's not fair," Luke said. His voice got low and tight. "That isn't fair! You don't have any idea what this—" He stuck his right hand in Lucy's face and splayed out the stumps. Lucy jerked her head back. "—is like. No idea! But you're smart and you're pretty, and you talk to me and then you're quiet at all the right times. . . . Do you remember that first day in the dining room?"

The scene flashed into Lucy's head. She recalled catching sight of Luke's hand for the first time, and the shock that he'd seen on her face.

"Of course," Lucy said quietly. "I'm terribly embarrassed about that."

"And yesterday in the woods," Luke went on. "Did you think I didn't know it made your skin crawl when I touched you?"

Lucy looked up at him. "I'm sorry, but I think you're exaggerating," she said. "Your hand just takes some getting used to. Other people wouldn't focus on your hand if *you* didn't. Maybe you need to just get over the past and move on with your life!"

Luke lowered his hand and shook his head. "You don't know what you're talking about." His eyes burned into hers for a moment more, then he turned and disappeared into the darkness.

TEN

Back at the campfire, Simon was pulling out the second letter from Beatrice's aunt.

"Excuse me," Simon said. "Could I bother everyone for a moment?"

"What's up, partner?" asked one of the hands.

"Do any of you know what the stream of green is?" Simon asked.

There was silence for a moment as the men thought. "Doesn't ring a bell with me," said one of the hands.

Another one was shaking his head. "'Stream of green . . .' Nope, I'm sorry, son. Never heard of it."

Simon was getting ready to give up when Old Ben, the hand who had ridden with Lucy, spoke up. "I haven't heard that name used in a long time," he said. "A very long time."

"You know of it, then?" Simon asked.

"Oh, yes," Ben said. "It's an old name for the stream that borders the southern pasture. Up until sixty years or so ago the stream always looked kind of green because of all the algae in it. At some point, somebody cleaned it up, and the name went the way of the water's color. It vanished!"

Simon was getting excited. "The southern pasture . . . ," he said. "Isn't that where we're going tomorrow?"

Ben grinned. "Sure is."

"*Yahoo!*" Simon crowed. He was one step closer to the treasure!

The next morning the group got up before dawn again. The reverend was putting on his boots outside his tent when he suddenly started screaming and hopping up and down.

"There's a snake in my boot!" he yelled. Cody immediately ran over to help.

"Don't worry," Cody said as he looked first in one boot, then the other, "this snake isn't poisonous. But the scorpion in your other boot is. Always check your boots in the morning, Reverend, or you won't be around long enough to rope any dogies." He walked away from camp and emptied both of the boots before giving them back to the reverend with a grin.

They reached the southern pasture by late morning. Mr. Henderson and a couple of the hands started through the herd, taking a count to make sure they hadn't lost any cattle. Meanwhile, Reverend Camden got started making lunch.

Simon was eager to check out the stream of green. Old Ben pointed toward a single oak tree standing on the other side of the pasture.

"The stream runs right beside that tree," Ben said.

"Thanks," said Simon. He mounted up. Ruthie and Cody went with him, and they cantered across the pasture. When they got to the stream, they dismounted and let their horses graze.

The stream was unremarkable—shallow and rocky. It didn't look green at all.

"Where would Beatrice's aunt hide something?" Cody asked.

Simon stood with his hands on his hips, looking up and down the stream. "If I were going to hide a treasure, I'd put it somewhere out of the way, where no one would stumble across it by accident. It would also have to be someplace that wouldn't change, maybe for a long time."

"It can't be *in* the stream, right?" Cody asked.

"I wouldn't think so," said Simon.

"What about in the tree?" Ruthie asked.

The three of them forded the stream and stood by the trunk of the tree. It was huge and looked as if it had been there forever. They circled the trunk. Ruthie scrutinized the roots while Simon and Cody peered up into the boughs.

"What about that hole?" Cody asked.

"Where?" said Simon.

Cody pointed. Halfway between the ground and the lowest branches was a dark hole in the side of the trunk.

"Yeah," Simon said. "I'll bet that's it!"

Simon wrapped his arms around the trunk and, pushing with his legs, began to shinny up the tree. When he got to the hole in the trunk, he carefully peered inside. He couldn't see anything.

"I'm sticking my hand in!" he called down.

"Watch out for spiders!" Ruthie called back.

"Thanks a lot," Simon said under his breath. Gripping the tree tightly with his legs, he slowly reached inside the hole.

Ick! he thought. *Lots of spiderwebs! And something furry!* Simon yanked his hand out of the hole just as an angry squirrel came charging out. Simon almost fell in surprise, but managed to recover his balance just in time.

With the squirrel gone and his position secured, Simon reached into the hole again. When his arm was about halfway into the hole, his fingers touched something hard and cool. It had edges and corners. . . .

"Yes!" Simon said. "I got it!"

Ruthie and Cody cheered. Simon grabbed the box and carefully removed it. It was made of tin and looked just like the first one.

"Here!" Simon called. "I'm going to drop it. Stand back!"

Simon let go of the box. It dropped to the

ground and bounced without opening. As quickly as he could, Simon climbed back down.

The three of them crouched around the box. Simon released the catch, and the box popped open.

"Another letter!" Cody said.

"Duh!" said Ruthie.

"Be nice," Simon said, carefully removing the letter. He unfolded it.

> *Dearest Beatrice,*
>
> *Remember how you used to hide things in that hole? I thought I would hide something for you. Thank you for being patient with me. I needed to be sure no one but you would find these notes.*
>
> *But there will be no more notes. Our treasured family heirloom awaits you . . . at home! Look under the blue step beneath the stairs.*
>
> *Keep it safe, and God bless you.*
> *Your loving Aunt*

"After all that," Simon said, "it's back at the house!"

Cody peered down at the words. *Under*

the blue step beneath the stairs . . .

"Does it make any sense to you?" Simon asked.

Cody shook his head. "I've never seen a blue step in the house before."

"Well, nothing to do but go and look for it," said Simon.

The three crossed back over the stream, mounted up, and rode back to the camp. When they got there, Simon was surprised to find Luke mounted up again—shouting at Mr. Henderson!

"It's your fault!" Luke was saying. "These people don't know how to run cattle. And now *I* have to make up for *their* mistakes!"

Before his father could respond, Luke spun his horse and galloped away. As Simon watched, Lucy swung up into Sunset's saddle and took off after Luke.

"Lucy!" the reverend called after her.

Mrs. Camden put her hand on her husband's arm. "Let her go," she said.

Simon dismounted and hurried over to the chuck wagon. Mr. Henderson was already there, talking to the reverend and Mrs. Camden.

"I'm so sorry," Mr. Henderson said. "I'm not sure what to do."

"We understand," said Mrs. Camden. "Maybe Lucy can help."

Mr. Henderson glanced at Simon, then tipped his hat and walked over to talk to some of the hands.

"What's going on?" Simon asked.

The reverend took a frothing pot of beans off the stove. "Looks like we lost a cow," he said.

"Is that it?" Simon asked. "I mean, I'm sure that's serious, but—"

"Luke blamed it on us," Mrs. Camden interrupted.

"Why'd he do that?" Ruthie asked.

The reverend poured out the beans. "I'm not sure, Ruthie. It's complicated."

Mrs. Camden looked off the way Luke and Lucy had gone. "Let's just hope Lucy can help him."

Sunset was huffing as she galloped across the grass. Lucy was hanging on to the horse's mane for dear life. Just ahead of them, also traveling at a gallop, were Luke and his horse.

Lucy was petrified. She'd never ridden a

horse so fast before! She felt as if she were barely hanging on. But as fast as Sunset was running, Luke was gradually pulling away from them.

Luke glanced back, then spurred his horse on. He meant to leave Lucy behind.

"Luke!" Lucy called. She didn't know if he could hear her over the pounding hooves.

He doesn't care, Lucy told herself. *Why are you trying so hard?*

Because he needs a friend, she answered herself. *Even though he doesn't want one, he needs one.* But that wasn't going to matter if she couldn't get him to slow down, because she wasn't going to be able to catch him.

They passed through a stand of cotton-wood trees, and Lucy ducked as she whizzed under a low branch. Suddenly she had an idea.

That's a really bad idea, she thought. It was dangerous. If she got hurt, she was trusting him to stop and help her.

But if she was going to do something, she had to do it soon. Luke was pulling farther and farther ahead. They were approaching another group of trees. Lucy glanced down. Why did the ground seem so far away?

Because it is far away! she thought.

Lucy unclamped one hand from Sunset's mane and grabbed the reins. As she and Luke passed beneath the trees, Lucy pulled back gently, slowing her horse. Taking a deep breath, she let go of the reins, reached up with both hands, and grabbed on to a branch.

She hit the branch hard enough to knock the wind out of her, but she managed to hold on. Sunset continued down the path, leaving Lucy hanging from the branch. Lucy dangled for a moment, then let go.

The ground rose up much more quickly than she'd expected. She screamed as she hit the dirt and twisted her ankle. All she could hear was the thud of hooves. . . .

When she opened her eyes, she was lying flat on her back. Her ankle was killing her.

She groaned.

"Lucy?"

Luke? The first thing she saw was the silhouette of a tree against the bright sky. Then Luke's head moved into her field of vision. His brow was furrowed with concern.

"You fell off Sunset," he said. "Are you all right?"

At least it worked, Lucy thought. She wet her lips. "I don't know," she croaked. "How do I look?"

"Not so great," he said, smiling slightly. "Your ankle is swollen, but I don't think it's broken."

Slowly, Lucy sat up. The pain in her ankle had subsided to a dull throb. Grazing nearby were Sunset and Luke's horse.

"What happened?" Luke wanted to know.

"I wasn't catching you on horseback, so I thought I'd try running instead," she answered glibly, silently asking Luke's forgiveness for lying to him.

Luke smiled again and shook his head. Seeing him smile was almost worth twisting her ankle.

"Are you sure you're okay?" he asked.

"I think so," Lucy answered, seriously this time. She flexed her ankle slightly. "Yeah, it's not bad. Just let me sit here for a minute."

Luke nodded and sat back on his heels. "I'm sorry," he said.

Lucy looked up in surprise. "For what?" she asked.

"For running from you," he said. "For

blaming you and your family for the lost cow." He rubbed his face with his hands. "Sometimes I can be pretty stupid."

"Yeah," Lucy agreed. "You can."

Luke chuckled. "Gee, thanks," he said.

"You're welcome," said Lucy.

They were quiet. Lucy drew up her legs, then closed her eyes and rested her forehead against her knees.

"I'm sorry, too," Lucy finally said.

Now Luke was surprised. "For what?"

"For being such a busybody and thinking I could solve all your problems. Maybe I should have just minded my own business. But you're just so cute, you see. . . ."

Lucy glanced up. Luke was smiling. "Yeah, that must make it pretty hard," he said, shaking his head.

Lucy reached out and smacked him on the shoulder. "And you're humble, too."

They were quiet for a while longer, then Lucy stretched out her leg. "I think I'm ready to travel," she said.

"Here," said Luke, holding out a canteen. Lucy gratefully took a drink and handed it back.

Luke took a drink, too, then screwed on the cap. "So, do you want to come with me to find this cow? I promise, we'll take it slow."

"No galloping?" Lucy asked.

Luke shook his head. "No galloping."

"In that case, I accept."

Luke helped her to her feet and supported her as she limped over to the horses. His arm felt warm around her waist.

"Where are we going to look?" Lucy asked. She bent her knee, and Luke boosted her up into Sunset's saddle.

"We'll retrace the path we took with the herd," Luke said, walking over to his own horse. "I think I've got a pretty good idea where that cow is."

Together, they started riding back along the trail. As they rode, Luke paused often to scrutinize the plants and bushes they passed, looking for signs that the cow had been there. As it turned out, they didn't need the signs.

"What's that?" Lucy asked.

"What?" asked Luke.

Lucy waited until she heard it again. "That."

Luke lifted his head and listened. Then he heard it, and his eyes widened in surprise.

It sounded like a horn, or maybe a bull-frog croaking. Judging by the expression on Luke's face, Lucy didn't think it was either of those.

"Come on," Luke said, leading the way. Following the sound, they eventually topped a rise and started down into a slight hollow surrounded by scrub brush. There, standing with its head hanging near the ground, was the missing cow.

As Lucy watched, the cow raised its head slightly and let out the low bellow they'd been hearing. "Is it in pain?" Lucy asked. "What's wrong with it?"

Luke dismounted and hurried over to the cow. "Yeah, it's in pain, all right," he said. He eased his way carefully around the cow and peered at its rear end. Then he looked at Lucy. "This cow is about to have a calf!"

ELEVEN

Lucy's jaw dropped. "What?" she finally said.

"Come here," Luke said. "I'm going to need your help."

Lucy carefully dismounted and limped over to Luke and the cow. The cow was breathing heavily, and its eyes looked wild.

"I think there's something wrong," Luke said. "It's not usually this hard for them."

"What do we do?" Lucy asked.

Luke looked at her. "You don't want to know," he said as he started rolling up his sleeves.

Suddenly realizing what Luke was about to do, Lucy put a hand on the cow's shoulder to steady herself. "What do you want *me* to do?"

"Stay up by her head," Luke said. "Hold it. She'll probably try to reach back here and bite me."

Great, Lucy thought. *So she'll bite me instead?*

But she didn't say that. Now was not the time. Instead, she wrapped her arms around the cow's head and hung on.

"Okay, here I go," Luke said.

A moment later, the cow bellowed and jerked its head up, banging Lucy's chin.

"Ouch!" she said, leaning into the cow. *"This thing is strong!"*

She could barely see Luke behind the cow, working for what seemed like hours. Finally, he said, "There it is. . . . I've got it. . . ."

Then there was a sound like water splattering on concrete, and all the tension went out of the cow's neck.

"You can let her go, Lucy," Luke said.

She did, and the cow immediately turned around and began licking the wet, sticky calf behind it.

"Wow!" Lucy said. "You did it!"

Luke had a pleased expression on his face. "Yeah, I did, didn't I?"

After Luke had washed his hands in a nearby pond, they watched the mother and calf together. After ten minutes, the calf was on its feet and feeding. It was wobbly, soft, and adorable!

"Now what?" Lucy asked. She looked up at the sky. She didn't think it could be much later than one o'clock.

"I don't know about you," Luke said, "but I'm starving."

"Me too," said Lucy, suddenly aware of her growling stomach. "Is this little guy ready to travel?"

"Let's find out," Luke said. He got a coil of rope from his saddle and tied a noose around the mother cow's neck. The other end he tied to his saddle horn.

Luke boosted Lucy up to her saddle, then mounted up himself. They started back toward the camp at a walk. The mother cow ambled along behind them. Behind her walked her brand-new baby.

It took them an hour to get back to camp. When they arrived, everyone was astonished to see the new calf.

"No wonder she wandered off," Old Ben

said to Simon. "It looks like she had some business to take care of."

Before his father could ask him to, Luke apologized to Reverend and Mrs. Camden for being so rude. "I was completely out of line," he said, "and I'm sorry. Truth is, now that I look at her, I think that cow may have been my responsibility all along."

Lucy and Luke dove into some beans and started to tell the story about the calf's birth, but Ruthie interrupted. "Can we talk about this on the road?" she asked. "Simon's got a treasure to find!"

It was nearly dinnertime when they got back to the house. Everyone, including the cowhands, cleaned up and met in the dining room.

During dinner, everyone regaled Mrs. Henderson with stories of the trip—the reverend's burned beans, Ruthie's exciting moment, and Lucy and Luke's birthing of the calf.

Then it was Simon's turn to talk about what he'd found in the old tree by the stream of green. "Beatrice's aunt's last note says something about a blue step beneath the stairs." Simon looked at Mr. Henderson, then Mrs. Henderson. "Do you know what she's talking about?"

Mr. Henderson sat back and crossed his arms. Mrs. Henderson was shaking her head. "I'm afraid I don't, Simon," she said. "I don't know anything about a blue step. Do you, Cal?"

"No," Mr. Henderson said. "No, I don't, but that doesn't mean there wasn't one."

"What do you mean?" Simon asked.

"There's no telling how many times the steps have been painted, then sanded down, then painted again. But if Beatrice's aunt hid something under the steps, blue or no, I'd think it'd still be there. Don't you, Rachel?"

Mrs. Henderson was nodding now. "I think so. Shall we go have a look?"

"I don't see why not," said Mr. Henderson. "We'll be ripping those stairs up any day now anyway."

Luke fetched a couple of crowbars and hammers and everyone met next to the stairs. Some of the hands pitched in, and before long they'd removed the tops of three of the steps.

Cody ran and got a flashlight, and Simon shined it into the space under the stairs. He was quiet for a while, flicking it back and forth. Finally, he stepped back, chagrined.

"I don't see anything," he said.

"Mind if I have a look?" Mr. Henderson asked.

Simon handed him the flashlight, and Mr. Henderson peered around. He stepped back. "Well, I hate to do it, Simon, but I'm going to have to agree with you. Ain't nothin' down there but a whole lot of cobwebs."

Disappointed, the group put the steps back so the Camdens could get up to their rooms that night.

It was hard to tell who was more dejected, Simon or Ruthie. "And after we got so far," Simon lamented.

Mr. Henderson shook his head. "Maybe Beatrice's aunt never got a chance to hide the treasure. Or maybe her son found it and sold it."

Mr. Henderson shrugged, but then Old Ben spoke up. "Wait a minute, now. Wait just a minute. How old is this house?"

"Relatively new, given the history of the ranch," said Mrs. Henderson. "Maybe sixty or seventy years old? Why?"

It hit Lucy and Luke at the same moment. "The old homestead!" they cried.

"What?" Simon said.

Lucy suddenly blushed. She'd forgotten that she hadn't told anyone about Luke's taking her there. Luke explained for her. "What's left of the old homestead is a few miles west of here. I'll bet *that's* the staircase Beatrice's aunt is talking about!"

"Of course!" said Mrs. Henderson. "This house wasn't even built when Beatrice's aunt was alive."

Mrs. Camden was looking at her watch. "Normally I would say we should wait until morning to check this out, but—"

"But this is too darned exciting!" finished the reverend. "I say we saddle up!"

TWELVE

Everyone cheered and hurried to get ready for the ride out to the homestead. Cody produced flashlights for everyone, and Mr. Henderson and Luke took a couple of shovels and crowbars. The cowhands wished them luck on their search and left to go home to their families. Then the Camdens and Hendersons saddled up and rode out to the woods where the old foundation was. It was a bright night—the moon was nearly full—but they still took it slow. When they reached the woods, they dismounted and turned on their flashlights.

"Too dark in there to stay on horseback," Mr. Henderson said. He winked at Lucy. "Don't want anyone to run into a branch and get knocked off her horse."

They walked their horses through the woods, their flashlights playing over the trees. When they reached the clearing, they tethered the horses and walked among the sprawling stones.

"Where would the front steps have been?" Simon asked aloud.

"Somewhere near the front door?" Luke guessed.

"But where was that?" asked Ruthie.

They walked among the ruins in silence, shining their flashlights over everything, until Cody called out, "I think I found them!"

Everyone congregated around the young boy.

"I think you *have* found them, Cody," said Mr. Henderson. At the base of a partial piece of wall was a single rotted board that could very well have been a step.

"So if the steps went up here . . . ," Simon said.

". . . that means the treasure would be somewhere along this wall!" Ruthie said.

Simon hefted a shovel. "Nothing to do but look," he said.

Everyone took turns clearing away leaves and poking around in the dirt. They found all sorts of pieces of stone, and Lucy found a piece of wood that looked as if it might have been painted blue a long time ago. But it was Simon who finally found the treasure.

He and Luke were poking around when Simon's shovel made a clinking noise. Everyone froze.

"Was that . . . ," Mrs. Camden began.

Simon put his shovel aside, got down on his hands and knees, and began clearing away the dirt.

"There's something here," he said. He cleared away more dirt, then picked up the same sort of box that had held the clues.

Everyone crowded around Simon and Luke and focused their flashlights on the object in the box.

"Is that silver?" Reverend Camden said.

"I think I see turquoise!" said Mrs. Camden.

When Simon removed the object from the box, they saw a beautifully made necklace of silver and turquoise. For a moment, they all just admired it.

"And to think we found this because of your detective work, Simon!" said Mr.

Henderson. "Not too bad for a part-time rancher!"

"Yeah, Simon," said Luke, glancing at Lucy. "Nice work."

Simon looked bashful. "I like puzzles," he said. "I only hope it's worth something."

Mrs. Henderson was examining it now. "Something as old as this? And I wonder who made it? It looks like it might be Navajo work."

Mr. Henderson was nodding. "Simon, this'll bring in a pretty penny, I'm sure."

"*If* we decide to sell it," said Mrs. Henderson. "After all, look at the lengths Beatrice's aunt went to to save it from being sold!"

"You're right," said Mr. Henderson. "It might be doing a disservice to our family to sell it. It's an heirloom, right?"

"Right!" the other Hendersons chimed in.

"Ruthie, are you all packed?" Mrs. Camden asked.

"Yes, Mom," Ruthie replied.

It was the Camdens' last day at the ranch. Though the Hendersons had invited them to stay as long as they liked, the

Camdens did not want to overstay their welcome. Checking out the old homestead and finding the lost necklace seemed a good way to end their visit. Plus, the bunkhouse Mrs. Camden had been working on was finished! The Hendersons had agreed it was a perfect model for the rest of the bunkhouses.

It promised to be another beautiful day, clear and hot. Lucy sighed and flexed her ankle, which was feeling better but was still stiff. The last few days had been amazing, full of incredible experiences. She was sad to be leaving. And she hadn't seen Luke this morning. He hadn't even showed up to help feed the horses. She couldn't shake the nasty suspicion that he was avoiding her.

Then she heard the sound of gravel crunching beneath tires. She looked over and saw the ranch truck coasting to a stop beside the porch. Behind the wheel was . . . Luke!

"Hey!" Lucy called. She started down the steps.

"Hey," Luke said. He grinned at her as she limped over to the truck.

"What are you up to?" Lucy asked, resting her arms in the truck's open window.

Luke nodded toward the road. "Just going up the road a piece, to repair a section of fence. It'll only take a little bit. Want to come along?"

"Are you kidding?" Lucy asked. She swung open the door and hopped up into the cab. "Let's go!"

"Yeehaw!" Luke called as they tore around the drive and up the road.

They stopped about five minutes from the house to work on a small section of fence. Lucy knew what she was doing now and worked at the same time as Luke; he took the top wire, and she took the bottom.

They worked silently and quickly. Lucy was aware of how close they were. Unlike the last time they had mended the fence, they brushed against each other as they worked, touching hands as they exchanged tools.

When they were finished, they stood back to admire their work.

"Miss Lucy," Luke said, "you can be a hand on my ranch anytime."

Lucy smiled at him. Looking him in the eye, she reached out and took his right hand gently in hers. "Thank you," she said.

Leaving his injured hand where it was,

Luke reached up with his good hand and touched Lucy's cheek. Then he leaned in and gave Lucy a kiss that she felt all the way down to the tips of her toes.

When they parted, Luke blushed.

Lucy smiled. "What is it?" she asked.

Luke sighed. "This kind of thing is hard for me, but I just wanted to say how much I appreciate your not giving up on me, no matter how mean I was. You stuck it out. That means a lot."

He took his right hand from Lucy's and flexed it. He shook his head.

Lucy reached out and took his hand again. She gave it a squeeze. It still felt a little weird to her, but that didn't matter to either of them.

"You've got nothing to be ashamed of," Lucy said.

Luke smiled. He leaned down and kissed her again. "Thank you, Miss Lucy Camden," he said.

They rode back to the ranch holding hands across the truck's bench seat, letting go only when they got near the house.

Out front, the reverend had pulled the Camdens' car around. Simon was helping him load it up. The rest of the family was standing around, talking to the Hendersons.

Once the car was loaded, they all said their goodbyes.

"We're sure sorry to see you Camdens go," said Mr. Henderson. "You know you have an open invitation to come here anytime."

"That's right," said Mrs. Henderson. "And next time, Reverend, you don't have to cook!"

"Okay," said the reverend, "but next time, you don't feed us for free, either."

The Hendersons smiled. "Fair enough," said Mr. Henderson.

"Mount up!" the reverend called.

Bidding their farewells, the Camdens climbed into the car and turned to go down the driveway. Mr. and Mrs. Henderson, Luke, and Cody watched them go.

"When we come next summer, I want to stay in the bunkhouse I helped rebuild," said Mrs. Camden.

"When?" said the reverend.

"Uh-huh," Mrs. Camden replied.

"Yeah!" said Ruthie.

Simon and Lucy nodded. "Definitely," they said.

The reverend sighed. "Okay," he said. "Hey, does that mean you guys feel like having beans for dinner tonight?"

There was a moment of shocked silence before cries of "No way!" "Are you crazy?" "Not on your life!" and "Forget it!" filled the car.

The reverend laughed as he turned off the ranch's private drive onto the main road.

They passed the sign for the ranch. Lucy looked through the rear window and smiled. They'd be seeing the Lucky Star Dude Ranch again.

DON'T MISS THIS BRAND-NEW, ORIGINAL COLLECTION OF FUN, FALL 7TH HEAVEN STORIES!

RUTHIE GOES TO HOLLYWOOD

Ruthie is off to Hollywood! She's won an all-expenses-paid trip—*and* a walk-on role in her favorite television show! But her mother, the *chaperone*, seems bent on spoiling all the fun.

THE BEST OKTOBERFEST

Robbie and Simon are representing the church in the annual Oktoberfest games—and they plan to win! Simon's rivalry with the Doubler twins has been going on for years, but this year's competition has an unexpectedly romantic twist. . . .

SISTERS THROUGH THE SEASONS

Lucy and Mary are testing their survival skills—in New York City! A pre-Christmas shopping trip sounds harmless enough, but the Big Apple has more bite than the girls bargained for!

ISBN: 0-375-82290-9

7th Heaven
SISTERS THROUGH THE SEASONS

Featuring **3** original stories!

Based on
the hit TV series
created by
Brenda Hampton

DON'T MISS THIS BRAND-NEW, ORIGINAL 7TH HEAVEN STORY

Now Available!

WINTER BALL

Lucy Camden is going to her first college dance—a charity ball. She's got the dress, she's got the date, but she's also got a problem. She wants to be as popular in college as she was in high school, and she's on her way. She's even been appointed to the winter ball's planning committee. Unfortunately, the plans being made may break the law. If Lucy objects, the whole ball could be ruined, as well as her social life. Now Lucy's got a choice to make: accept the party line or wreck everyone's party time.

Available wherever books are sold!
ISBN: 0-375-81430-2

DON'T MISS THIS BRAND-NEW, HEARTWARMING COLLECTION OF ORIGINAL 7TH HEAVEN STORIES

Now Available!

LUCY'S
ANGEL

While visiting her grandfather in Arizona, Lucy Camden uncovers a beautiful angel ornament in his basement—one that seems to have a magical message. Meanwhile, flying home from Buffalo proves disastrous for Mary. When an unexpected blizzard forces her to camp out on the floor of an airport terminal, she wonders what could be worse? Then Matt picks up a stranded motorist on his way to a swingin' New Year's Eve in Las Vegas. But the trouble is that this impersonator thinks he's actually *Elvis*!

DON'T MISS THIS BRAND-NEW, ORIGINAL 7TH HEAVEN STORY

Now Available!

CAMP CAMDEN

Lucy and Ruthie are off to summer camp in sunny Malibu, California, where swimming, boating, and horseback riding aren't their only pastimes! Lucy's teaching a class that catches the attention of a handsome counselor, and Ruthie is pulling pranks that make everyone take notice! Meanwhile, back at the Camden house, Simon's trying his latest moneymaking scheme—day-trading on the Internet! But is the stock market ready for Simon Camden?

Available wherever books are sold!
ISBN: 0-375-81360-8